To: The
Holy Cro

I hope you enjoy this
novel about Christianity
in Ancient Rome!.
Mary-Ellen

St. George's
Mysterious Cross

St. George's Mysterious Cross

M.E. Bergvinson

Copyright © 2012, M.E. Bergvinson

All rights reserved. No part of this book may be reproduced, stored, or transmitted by any means—whether auditory, graphic, mechanical, or electronic—without written permission of both publisher and author, except in the case of brief excerpts used in critical articles and reviews. Unauthorized reproduction of any part of this work is illegal and is punishable by law.

ISBN 978-1-300-13979-9

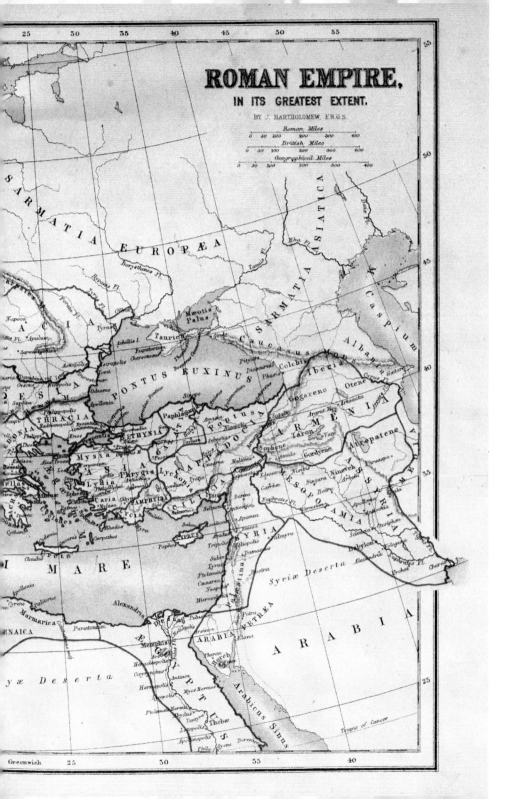

ROMAN EMPIRE,
IN ITS GREATEST EXTENT.

BY J. BARTHOLOMEW, F.R.G.S.

Roman Miles
0 50 100   200   300   400

British Miles
0 50 100   200   300   400

Geographical Miles
0 50   100   200   300   400

Mary-Ellen Bergvinson was born in 1969 in London, Ontario. She graduated from Carleton University with a B.A. in Sociology/Anthropology. Currently she resides in Courtenay, British Colombia, with her husband and four sons.

For Joseph, Thomas, Markus and Lukas

A NOTE

St. George is one of the world's best-loved saints, despite the fact that his true identity remains largely a mystery. Unlike most other saints, whose biographies and accomplishments have been accurately recorded and passed down over the centuries, George has gone down in history as the saint who killed a dragon. No wonder some people believe he's nothing more than a myth. When I first read the legend of St. George and the dragon, I was intrigued. I wanted to learn more about the man behind the armour. Who was he? I wondered. And what was it about him that's inspired generations of people from around the globe to spin tales about his bravery, give metals in his honour, and build churches in his name?

Early into my research I became equally fascinated with the era in which he lived, a period at the beginning of the fourth century known as the Great Persecution. The exact number of Christians tortured and killed during this persecution is unknown; however, Christianity not only survived, it emerged from the fourth century as the dominant religion of the Western world. According to scholars, the fourth century is one of the most important periods of social change in the history of Western civilization, yet most people know little about it. Popular culture provides loads of information on the time of Jesus and the Middle Ages (when Christian kings and queens ruled the Western world), but what happened in between? How did we get from point A to point B?

In this story I've attempted to weave together most of the folklore and information surrounding St. George's life and death, along with some important historic figures and events of the time. I've included a partial bibliography for reference and would especially like to thank The Teaching Company for providing so many great courses. I'd also like to thank Terry Penney for his help with the cover photo.

M.E. Bergvinson

(I)

"Hurry!" hollered Daniel. "It's leaving!"

He threw his shoulder into the heavy glass door and waited, one foot in the building and one out, ready to make a run for it. *If Steve doesn't get here soon...*

Bang! Somewhere down the long, crowded corridor of the school a locker door slammed shut.

"Wait up!" called Steve. "I'm coming!"

Seconds later, Daniel's best friend came into view, his open backpack swinging from one hand, his coat from the other.

Without a second glance, Daniel took off flying down the icy front steps two at a time, almost knocking over a couple of eighth grade girls in the process.

"Hey! Watch it!" one of them scowled, but he didn't have time to slow down. If he and Steve missed their bus, it'd be forever before one of their parents could pick them up, and hanging around the school after hours on a Thursday was not his idea of a good time, especially on a day like today.

With Steve close on his heels, he jumped the last four stairs and sprinted along the bustling sidewalk toward Bus Number 33, which sat idling at the front of the line, its doors already closed in preparation for departure. Gasping for breath, he reached the bus just as it started to pull away from the curb.

"Archie!" he shouted, peering through the folding door at the driver and waving his arms in desperation. "Stop!" But Archie was looking in the opposite direction, his eyes glued to the rear-view mirror, checking to see that the coast was clear.

Steve skidded to a halt next to Daniel and pounded on the door until the noise caught the attention of the chubby girl with glasses who always sat in the seat directly behind Archie. She reached over and tapped him on the shoulder, motioning in their direction.

The bus came to an abrupt stop, and seconds later Daniel and Steve collapsed gratefully into a couple of seats near the front, alongside some of the other students they'd come to know during their first year of junior high.

"What took you guys so long?" asked Kate.

"Mr. Darkangelo," panted Daniel, peeling off his favourite toque and shaking the hair from his eyes. "He asked Steve to stay after class so that he could talk to him about the World Religions assignment that's due after the break."

"Oh, that," groaned Kate.

"I thought you were going away for the Easter break," said the boy across the aisle. He was only one year older than the others but you'd never know it; his long legs stretched out several feet into the aisle.

"I am," muttered Steve, tugging at the zipper of his over flowing backpack. Eventually he gave up and dropped it carelessly onto the floor next to his feet. "But apparently Mr. Darkangelo doesn't understand the concept of the word *holiday*. As if I'm going to work on an essay while I'm in Disneyland."

"Don't worry about it," said the long-legged boy. "At least you're going somewhere. Hey," he turned toward the freckly, red headed boy seated next to the window, "aren't you going away too?"

"Yeah...to Cuba!" his wide smile exposed a mouth full of braces. "I leave tomorrow!"

"Must be nice," said Long Legs enviously. "How about you Daniel? What are you doing for the holidays?"

Daniel shrugged his shoulders. "Nothin' much."

The truth was that early the next morning Daniel would be heading to his grandparent's farm for the two-week break. His parents had promised to take him skiing but as usual had cancelled at the last minute due to an unexpected business trip. Daniel was disappointed about the change of plans, but he figured that going to the farm would be more exciting than staying home for the Easter break, especially since Steve would be in Disneyland. Two weeks can drag by pretty slowly when the bulk of your time is torn between watching TV and playing video games; massive boredom sets in by about day two. Besides, the farm wasn't too bad. His Grandpa usually managed to find ways to keep him entertained. In fact, the last time they'd talked, he'd mentioned something about a surprise. Daniel was kind of curious to find out what that was all about. Even so, he didn't see the point in mentioning his vacation plans to his friends. Feeding a bunch of cows and playing checkers was hardly what most thirteen year olds would consider a good time.

"Well, look on the bright side," teased the redheaded boy, "you'll have plenty of time to get Mr. Darkangelo's assignment done."

"Thanks," said Daniel, "that makes me feel much better."

"What's the assignment?" asked Long Legs.

"Five hundred words on the religious historic figure of your choice," said Steve, imitating Mr. Darkangelo.

Long Legs feigned a wide yawn.

"Tell me about it," said Kate. "I have no idea who I'm going to do mine on…maybe Ghandi. Would he count?"

"I don't know," said Steve. "But if I don't get something on paper by the time I get back, I'm definitely going to have to do summer school." He looked up at the ceiling and groaned at the thought of it.

"Why don't you get Daniel to do it for you," came an unexpected voice. "He's an expert on religion."

Simultaneously, all heads spun in the direction of the voice. Seated directly behind them, in his usual position, with his back against the window and his right leg stretched out comfortably on his chair, sat Ralph, a beefy eighth grader with no neck and a face like a bull dog. Unlike the rest of the kids, he rarely had to share his spot. Over the years he'd earned a well-deserved reputation as being an obnoxious bully, the type that people went out of their way to avoid. The other students would rather sit three to a seat than squished up next to him.

Steve cranked his neck around. "What?" he said in annoyance.

"I'm just sayin', since you're gonna be away, and since your buddy there," he jerked his head toward Daniel, "is a choir boy, why don't you just get him to do it for you?"

Daniel didn't know what Ralph was talking about, but he wished he'd shut up. At the sound of his loud voice, half of the students on the bus had turned to stare, including the cute blonde from music class. For weeks he'd been trying to get her to notice him, but this was not what he had in mind.

"What are you talking about?" he said defensively.

Ralph smiled. He loved to make people squirm. "Well, sooorrry if I got my church terms wrong. All I know is, last Christmas my Gran dragged me off to church and I saw you there, up on the stage, dressed in a pretty white dress, helping the priest."

Daniel felt his face turn bright red. Ralph had obviously seen him alter serving at the Christmas Eve Mass. If he wasn't so humiliated he'd have cracked a joke about Ralph's dim-witted misuse of the word "stage," but under the circumstances he didn't feel that this was the time to show off his familiarity with proper Church lingo. The others might get the wrong impression and think that he was some sort of religious freak.

"I don't know what you're talking about," he said.

"Yes, you do," insisted Ralph. "I know what I saw. You were up there praying and everything. So special…" he folded his hands together at his chest and made a face.

"No I wasn't," said Daniel, avoiding Steve's eye. The others might not know that he was lying, but Steve would. He'd been to Mass with Daniel a couple of times and knew that he sometimes served. Daniel hated having to lie; it made him feel like a real slug. But what choice did he have? As far as he was concerned, this was all his parents' fault. He'd told them that he didn't want to alter serve anymore, but they'd insisted. *They just don't understand how hard it is for kids nowadays,* thought Daniel. *Things are different than they used to be.* He knew lots of people who didn't go to church, let alone alter serve, and they seemed just fine, in fact, better than fine — they didn't get centered out and criticized by jerks like Ralph.

"Tell me, Ralph," said Long Legs with mock seriousness, "was this before or after Santa Claus landed on your roof?"

Everyone burst out laughing.

Thankful for the chance to blow Ralph off, Daniel quickly turned back around and asked Kate to tell him more about her new horse, a subject that he knew she never tired of. While she rambled on about her horse, he began to relax and let his mind drift. Before long he found himself wondering, once again, about the surprise that awaited him at the farm.

By the time he stepped off the bus, he'd decided that going to the farm wouldn't be so bad after all. It may not be the most adventurous or exotic of holidays, but it would still be a relaxing two-week break from school.

(II)

Daniel's grandparents lived on a farm outside of a sleepy town called Mayerthorpe. The locals called it Mudthorpe, though, because like most small towns in rural Alberta, the roads weren't paved. The springs were especially muddy. So early the next morning Daniel put on his rubber boots (but remembered to pack his winter boots because springs in northern Alberta are always very unpredictable) and hopped into his mother's minivan for the two-hour drive from Edmonton to his grandparents' farm.

He'd done this drive a million times before. Fields, cows, more fields...

After staring blankly out of his window for what seemed like hours, he plugged a movie into the van's overhead screen, and before he knew it, they were pulling off of the highway and onto the gravel road that led to the farm.

He straightened up in his seat and peered anxiously into the distance toward the long row of towering poplars that lined the edge of his grandparents' laneway. Through their leafless, swaying branches he caught a glimpse of the house, and for the first time in days his mood began to brighten. He loved the farm as though it were an old friend, loved everything about it: the chicken coop (empty now but for the family of barn cats that moved in last fall), the horses, the cattle, the dozens of barbed-wire fences that his grandfather always seemed to be mending, the gigantic vegetable garden, even the rusty antique tractor that was parked permanently behind the barn. As far back as he could remember he'd been visiting the farm, and in all that time it had never changed, a rare quality in this fast-paced world. Maybe that was why he loved it so much. While the outside world spun out of control, it remained consistent, predictable, a rock in an ever-changing sea of uncertainty.

The house itself was old, and some of its white paint was peeling away, but it was comfortable and sturdy and well built. It sat atop a high ridge overlooking the open prairie. In the front yard, there was an old spruce tree that was perfect for climbing. In the summertime, he could often be found sitting in its branches, gazing at the world, which lay stretched out before him, an endless sea of fields and aspen trees. It was the perfect spot to sit and watch the storms roll in. Only when the wind started to blow and big fat raindrops begin to fall would he run inside the house for shelter.

Like most of their neighbours, Daniel's grandparents were cattle farmers. Their more than two sections of land had at one time been home to over a hundred and fifty head of cattle, but over the past few years they'd scaled back considerably. They had decided, now that they were older, that they'd like more time to spend on the things they really enjoy, like riding horses and tending to their gardens. They now kept only a dozen cows, just enough to keep them busy during calving season.

As they drove up the laneway, Daniel watched the small group of cows grazing in the field with their newborn calves. The longer he watched them the more concerned he became. Something wasn't right; something was missing. He leaned forward and was about to share his concerns with his mother when their van suddenly came to a stop in front of the house. He glanced over his shoulder in time to see his grandmother emerge from the mudroom door and rush forward, eager to welcome them.

While Daniel's mother pulled his bags from the back of the van, his grandmother smothered him with hugs and kisses.

"Let me look at you," she said, holding him out at arms length. "I think you've grown a couple of inches! And look at your hair!" she said as she tussled it. "When was the last time you had it cut?"

Daniel shrugged and brushed the hair from his eyes.

His grandmother smiled at him adoringly. "Oh, it doesn't matter," she said, hugging him again. "You're still the most handsome boy around."

Daniel was always embarrassed when his grandmother fussed over him like this. Even so, he smiled good-naturedly and hugged her in return. Being an only child, as well as the only grandson on this side of the family, he was used to this type of treatment. He didn't believe that he was nearly as handsome as his grandmother said he was. In fact, he really felt that he was quite ordinary looking, with his brown hair and eyes to match. She wasn't exaggerating though when she said he'd grown a lot. He was now taller than most of his friends.

Just as the three of them were preparing to head indoors Grandpa emerged from the barn and called out to them, "Caroline! Daniel! Come here, I have a surprise for you!"

"Oh, yes," said Grandma, "I'd almost forgotten. He's been waiting anxiously for the two of you to arrive all morning."

Daniel and his mother headed to the barn together, both wondering what in the world Grandpa had in store for them. As they trudged through the mud and the slush, Daniel was glad that he'd decided to wear his rubber boots.

With his mother following close behind, he entered the warm barn and inhaled the familiar, sweet smell of hay and manure. It was dimmer than it had been outdoors, and it took his eyes a minute to adjust to the light. Peering into the far corner, he spotted a mare and her newborn foal lying together in the hay.

"Oh Dad, he's beautiful!" said his mother in a hushed voice. She spoke quietly, so as to avoid startling the two horses. "I had no idea that Lady was expecting. When did she foal?"

"Early this morning," replied his grandfather. "I never told you because I wanted it to be a surprise."

"So this is the surprise that you've been hinting at," said Daniel. "When we drove in I noticed that Lady wasn't grazing in the field with the cows like she usually is. I was worried about her. I should have known that she had something to do with the surprise!"

Grandpa chuckled and gazed lovingly at his horse. "Yes, she's just fine, and listen," he looked over at Daniel, "when the time comes, I'd like you to help me train this colt. He'll be yours to ride whenever you like."

"Thanks, Grandpa. That'd be great!"

Daniel's grandfather was a big, burly man with sandy brown hair, smiling eyes, and huge, calloused hands. Daniel had always enjoyed spending time on the farm with him, helping with the chores, horseback riding, or just sitting with him and exchanging jokes. When he was really young he used to tell everyone that when he grew up he wanted to be a farmer just like his Grandpa. Now he had no idea what he wanted to be when he grew up.

Grandpa bent low over his mare and gave her a gentle scratch on the back before rising stiffly to his full height.

"Well, we'd better leave these horses to rest for awhile," he said as he headed toward the door. "You have time to stay for a coffee, don't you, Caroline?"

"I'd love one," smiled Daniel's mother.

With one last look at the newborn foal, Daniel turned and followed his mother and grandfather out of the barn and toward the farmhouse.

(III)

"Do me a favour and pass me that big one, over there," said Daniel's grandmother, pointing toward a box.

She and Daniel were busy rearranging one of the spare bedrooms. For years now, it had been used as a storage room, but Grandma had decided that it was time to clean it out. They were sorting items into piles: some to keep, some to throw out, and some to donate to the Salvation Army. Outside, the wind howled.

The first few days of Daniel's visit had been warm and sunny, perfect weather for the Easter weekend. When they weren't at church celebrating the Triduum*, Daniel and his grandfather had kept busy helping one of the neighbours burn brush from some newly cleared land. Since the weather was so nice, and since Lady and her new foal were both in good health, Grandpa had decided to put them out to pasture. Daniel had helped spread out a large, round bale of hay for the two of them to bed down in. He'd also helped put out some hay for the cows to eat. But overnight a storm had blown in bringing with it snow and colder temperatures. Grandpa was

---

* The Thursday before Easter signals the end of Lent and the beginning of the Paschal Triduum which lasts three days. It includes the celebration of the last supper on the evening of Holy Thursday, the Passion of the Lord on Good Friday, and the celebration of the resurrection of Christ at the Easter Vigil on Holy Saturday and Easter Sunday.

now busy moving the horses back into the barn where they would be sheltered from the blustery weather. Inside, the woodstove kept Daniel and his grandmother warm and cozy.

"Well, I think we're almost done," said Grandma, as Daniel set the cardboard box down in front of her. She had just finished opening it and was about to start sifting through its contents when the phone rang.

"I'd better answer that," she said, rising to her feet and hurrying toward the door. "You can start going through this one if you like. I'll be back in a minute."

Daniel was enjoying helping his grandmother sort through her things. Every box contained a new treasure. They'd discovered old hats, jewelry, photos, and even letters written by distant relatives who had long since passed away. What made it most interesting were the stories that she shared as the two of them worked, especially the ones about his mother when she was his age.

As soon as his Grandma left the room, Daniel peered curiously into the box to see what was inside. The first thing that he noticed was a small, square, wooden box so plain and ordinary looking that he probably would have overlooked it if it weren't so ancient. He reached in and picked it up. It had a tiny metal clasp on the front that kept the lid shut tight. Carefully, he opened it and saw that it contained a silver cross and chain. There are times in your life when you see something and instantly you know that you must have it, that for some reason you were meant to have it. This is how it was for Daniel as he gazed at the cross. He longed to touch it but wasn't sure if he should. Just then his grandmother returned.

"How are you making out?" she asked.

Daniel closed the lid quickly and turned to face her. "Ok," he said guiltily. He wasn't sure if he should have opened the box without her permission. These were, after all, her private possessions.

"What have you found?" she asked, motioning to the wooden box in his hands.

"It's an old box." He hesitated before adding, "I opened it. It looks like a cross of some kind."

"A cross?" his grandmother repeated, perplexed. She had no idea what he was talking about. "Let me see, dear."

Daniel handed it over and watched as she opened it.

"Oh, my goodness!" she exclaimed, peering inside. "It's your grandfather's pendant!" She took it out and held it closer to her eyes to examine it. "Won't he be thrilled. He's been missing it for quite sometime." After examining it thoroughly she looked up into her grandson's watchful eyes. "Would you like to hold it?" she asked.

He nodded his head eagerly.

"Here you are," she said, handing it over gingerly "but please be careful. It's very old."

It was heavier than he expected. He held the cross in the palm of his hand and let the chain dangle from between his fingers. Years of neglect had left it looking slightly tarnished, but it was still impressive. All along its outer edge were ornate, abstract designs. It was different than most of the crosses he'd seen because the horizontal and vertical bars crossed each other in exactly the middle, like a plus sign. When he turned it over he was surprised to find an inscription in an unfamiliar language etched into the back.

Spera in Domino et fac bonum

"What does this mean?" he asked.

"What's that dear?" murmured his grandmother distractedly, her nose buried deep within the contents of a box.

"Here, on the back of the cross." He walked over and showed her the inscription.

"I'm afraid I'm not much help without my reading glasses," she said, peering at the inscription through squinted eyes, "but I think that's Latin."

Just then the oven timer began to beep loudly in the next room.

"Why don't you ask your grandfather about it when he comes in," she suggested, rising to her feet and brushing herself off. "I'm sure he'll know. In fact," she glanced at her watch, "he should be in soon. It's almost dinnertime. Come on, we'll finish this later. First let's see if we can't fill that bottomless pit of yours," she teased.

Daniel shoved the cross into the pocket of his jeans and followed his grandmother into the kitchen.

+

He had just finished putting more logs into the woodstove when his grandfather blew in from outside. After stomping the snow off his boots he removed them along with his coveralls.

"I haven't seen a spring storm like this for years," he said. "It's a good thing Daniel's here. We'll have someone to shovel us out in the morning." He smiled and winked at his grandson.

Daniel grinned. He was used to his grandfather's teasing.

"How are the horses?" asked Grandma anxiously. "Did you get them settled into the barn?"

"Yes, they'll be safe in there," said Grandpa reassuringly. As he spoke, a particularly strong gust of wind rattled the windows causing him to add, "as long as the wind doesn't blow the roof off the barn tonight."

Before long, the three of them were sitting down to one of Grandma's delicious home cooked meals. There were mashed potatoes with melted butter, peas and carrots, roast beef, gravy, and Yorkshire pudding. For dessert she'd baked two apple pies, Daniel's favourite.

Halfway through the meal, Daniel remembered the cross he had tucked away inside his pocket. Carefully he withdrew it and held it out for his grandfather to see.

"Look what we found," he announced.

"St. George's cross!" exclaimed his grandfather. "Where on earth did you find it?"

"Daniel came across it while we were cleaning out the back room," explained Grandma. "It was hidden in one of the boxes."

Grandpa reached across the table and clasped it in his hand. "Did you find anything with it?" he asked hopefully.

Daniel shook his head. "Just the old box that it came in."

Grandpa sighed and examined the cross thoughtfully. "This used to belong to your great-grandfather," he said. "When he passed away the nursing home gave us a couple of boxes of valuables that he'd kept with him. This was among them. It was always very special to him. When he was sent over from England, as an orphan, it was all he had. His mother had given it to him on her deathbed." He stared at it in silence for a moment before continuing. "This cross is older than you can imagine. It's been in our family for hundreds of years. According to your great-grandfather, and his father before him, it once belonged to St. George." He paused and looked up at Daniel. "You do know who St. George is, don't you?" he asked.

Daniel shook his head.

"You've never heard of him?!" said Grandpa incredulously. "You're kidding!" Before continuing, he pushed his plate aside and leaned back comfortably in his chair.

Daniel always enjoyed sitting around the dinner table with a full belly and a hot cup of tea, listening to his grandfather's stories. He scraped his plate clean and waited patiently for him to continue.

"Well, Daniel, according to legend, he was a fearless knight and dragon slayer. Tales of his bravery have been told throughout the ages, in many parts of the world. He is, by far, one of the most well-known saints. In fact, he's the Patron Saint of many countries, including England."

"A dragon-slayer!?" exclaimed Daniel, staring at the cross in wide-eyed disbelief. "But I thought that saints were just people who went to church and prayed a lot. I always thought they were kind of...I don't know...boring."

Grandpa chuckled. "Boring! Heavens no. There's nothing boring about the lives of the saints. When I was young I used to enjoy listening to stories about them. People don't talk about them near as much as they used to...it's too bad really..."

"Yes," agreed Grandma, rising from her chair to pour each of them a steaming cup of tea. "And people don't pray to them like they used to either...prayers of intercession, I mean," she added at the look of confusion on Daniel's face.

"What's a prayer of intercession?" he asked.

"That's when you ask a saint to pray for you," she explained. "You see, only God can answer our prayers, but the saints are our heavenly friends who'll say a prayer on our behalf if we ask them to. It used to be common practice for Christians to ask the saints for help, after all," she said, "two prayers are better than one."

She sat down and poured a bit of cream into her tea and offered some to Daniel. He nodded and held out his cup.

"Different saints are appealed to at different times, depending on the need," she continued. "For instance, I remember, whenever my mother lost something, which she was very prone to do, especially in those last years, bless her soul, she would pray to St. Anthony. Now… how did that go again…?" She looked over at Daniel's grandfather inquiringly.

"St. Anthony, St. Anthony," he recited, "please come round, something lost must be found."

Grandma smiled. "Yes! That's it!"

"And would she find what she'd lost?" asked Daniel, skeptically.

"Usually, yes!" said Grandma.

Grandpa chuckled. "Yes…but you know," he said, "the saints were often appealed to in more difficult times too…a loved one lost at sea…disease…famine…life was more difficult then…death was a very real threat…always looming…and people were inspired by the saints. It's important to remember that saints were once just ordinary people, like us…ordinary people whose faith in God led them to do extraordinary things. George was always particularly popular. The crusading knights used to cry out his name as they rode into battle. There's a famous story about him and his battle with the dragon. I'm sure we've got a copy of it around here somewhere, haven't we?" he asked Grandma.

"Oh, yes," she said, heading toward the sink with an armful of dirty dishes. "You stay put. I'll go and see if I can find it."

As soon as she'd left, Grandpa rose from his seat and went over to the woodstove to check on the fire. Daniel looked over curiously at the cross which now lay abandoned on the table next to his grandfather's empty placemat. It was face down, and he found himself staring, once again, at the mysterious inscription on the back.

"Grandpa," he asked, "what do those words, on the back of the cross, mean?"

"Words?" Grandpa swung the door shut on the woodstove and set the poker back in its holder before returning to his seat. "I don't recall any words." He picked up the cross and held it close to his eyes. "Oh yes," he said. "Now I remember. Psalm 37. Spera in Domino et fac bonum."

"What does it mean?"

"Trust in the Lord and do good." He handed the cross back over to Daniel. "Words to live by, son."

At that moment, Grandma reappeared carrying a large book, entitled *Dragon Legends*. "Here you go," she said, setting it down on the table in front of Daniel. "The legend of St. George. He was a saint, knight, and dragon killer all wrapped up in one. There's nothing boring about that."

Daniel opened the book to the correct page and read: *St. George: Martyr-Saint, died 303 A.D., feast day April 23rd.*

"Hey, his feast day is tomorrow!" he exclaimed before asking, "What does 'martyr-saint' mean?"

"A saint is a person who dedicated their life to God and to serving others," explained Grandpa. "A martyr-saint is one who died defending their faith."

"Oh," said Daniel.

While his grandmother puttered around, clearing the table and preparing three heaping portions of apple pie and vanilla ice cream, Daniel stared at the open book in his lap. Underneath the title was a large, colourful depiction of St. George, sitting astride a powerful white steed and stabbing a serpentine dragon with a long lance. In the picture, the lance appears to have been sent down from the heavens above, as though from God himself.

I wonder how he was killed? thought Daniel. *He was a knight, so maybe he died in battle...maybe he fought in the Crusades! During the Crusading Wars a lot of knights took up the cross and died in battle against the Muslims...but...no, that can't be because the Crusades weren't until medieval times. Islam didn't even begin until about the year 630 A.D. with the preaching of their prophet, Mohammad, and according to this, St. George died in 303 A.D. That was only three hundred years after Jesus walked the earth!*

Suddenly he was struck with a thought. "Hey!" he exclaimed. "I have an assignment due when I get back. I'm supposed to do a report on a religious historic figure. Do you think that I could do it on St. George?"

"Of course!" said Grandma. "I think that's a great idea."

Daniel turned his attention back to the book. As he pored over it's contents, his grandfather watched him in silence. He marveled at how much his grandson had grown. Before long he would be a man. On impulse he picked up the cross.

"How old are you now?" he asked.

Daniel looked up from the book. "I just turned thirteen."

"Thirteen!" exclaimed his grandfather. "Well then, I suppose you're old enough to appreciate a family heirloom. Would you like to have it?"

Daniel's face lit up. "Are you serious? Yeah, I'd like to have it!"

Grandpa smiled and handed it over to him. He knew how important it had been to his father and was glad to see that Daniel appreciated it so much. *After all*, he thought, *what good is it doing sitting in a box?* Still, he hoped that Daniel would treat it with the respect that it deserved; it contained powers that even he did not fully understand. It was this that prompted him to say, "Daniel, this is no ordinary pendant. I want you to promise me that you'll take very good care of it, and please...wear it wisely."

(IV)

Daniel's grandparents were in the habit of going to bed early, so while he was staying with them, Daniel often spent his evenings in bed, reading.

On this particular evening, after saying his goodnights, he headed up to his room with the legend of St. George tucked under one arm. He was looking forward to learning more about St. George and the dragon.

Before opening the book, he admired his new cross. Deciding that it needed a good cleaning, he found one of his grandmother's jewelry cloths and set about polishing it until it shined. When he was satisfied with the results, he set the cross down on his bedside table and picked up his book. He turned out the light, turned on his flashlight (while on the farm he liked to read by flashlight because it meant that he didn't have to climb out of bed again to turn out the lights), and began to read:

> Long ago, in a faraway land, there was a beautiful city called Silene that was besieged by an evil dragon.
>
> Silene was in an eastern province of the Roman Empire. Before the dragon appeared, the surrounding countryside was lush and fertile, with plentiful gardens and fruit orchards. Shepherds watched over their flocks peacefully in the meadows. Then, one dreadful afternoon, without warning and seemingly out of nowhere, it came.

At first it was nothing more than a mysterious black speck in the blue horizon. As it drew nearer people dropped what they were doing to gaze up at the sky in wonder. By the time its enormous, scaly body and bony, black wings could be distinguished it was too late for most; there was no escape. In one foul swoop the evil dragon began its reign of terror.

For weeks it pillaged the countryside, burning fields with its fiery breath and killing livestock. The villagers panicked. Most salvaged what they could and fled to the neighbouring kingdoms; those who didn't were killed. Eventually, only the king and the citizens of Silene remained. They were safe as long as they stayed within the walls of their gated city.

In the beginning, the dragon was satisfied to feed on grazing sheep and cows beyond the walls of the city. But after a time, it ran out of food. It was then that it began to circle the walls, sniffing at cracks and crevices with its scaly nose, seeking a way in. Those were dark days for the townsfolk. Not one of them was brave enough to try and slay the dragon. They feared that their weapons would be useless against the fiery breath and sharp claws of the awful beast.

In an attempt to appease the dragon, the king ordered his soldiers to tie two sheep to a post just outside of the city's gate. This was to be done early each morning, before sunrise, while the dragon lay sleeping in its lair.

This strategy worked well for a while, but eventually the citizens ran out of sheep. Again the putrid dragon began circling the walls of the city and clawing at the gate in search of a way in.

In desperation the king called all of his citizens to the town square. After much discussion it was decided that early each morning one person's name would be randomly drawn, as in a lottery. Whomever's name was drawn would be tied to the post for the dragon to feast upon, just as the sheep had been.

The days that followed were filled with much sorrow and tears as one by one the townsfolk were dragged off like sacrificial lambs to be fed to their beastly enemy, the dragon. And each afternoon the villagers helplessly gathered and mourned the deaths of their loved ones.

Early one morning, before the sun had begun to rise, the name chosen was that of the king's own daughter. Bravely the princess allowed herself to be adorned in a beautiful white gown and taken outside of the city's walls where she was tied to the post.

As she waited, alone, for that wretched dragon to arise from its slumber, she saw a man on horseback approaching at a distance. It was none other than the brave and handsome George, riding upon his valiant white steed. Although a Roman knight, he was a Christian; this she could tell by the cross that he bore. He was on a journey in search of adventure.

He approached the fair maiden, and she told him of her fate. She warned him that he must flee quickly, before the fearful dragon appeared and killed them both. But George was no coward; he refused to run and instead vowed to defeat the dragon and to rescue the princess from the throes of death.

In haste, he rode to where the dragon lay, still sleeping, in its lair. As he drew near, he was overwhelmed by the foul stench of the beast. But still he crept forward, quickly, lest the awful creature awaken and tear him to pieces with its dagger sized teeth. Its body was covered in a thick layer of scales, like a shield. George knew that his weapons would never penetrate such protective armour.

As he stood by, quietly watching and waiting, the dragon stirred and rolled over exposing its smooth belly. Without hesitation, he drew his lance and stabbed the beast with all of his force.

Putrid black blood gushed from its mortal wound. With an earth-shattering roar, the dragon reared onto its hind legs and blew searing hot fire from its nostrils. George jumped aside barely escaping the deadly flames.

Fearful of its impending death, the dragon fought with the fury of a caged animal. It thrashed its tail wildly sending boulders flying in all directions.

Through the ensuing battle, George refused to give in but instead brandished his sword and held his shield high. Weakened by its wound the dragon soon became feeble. It let out one last horrifying wail before it rolled over and died.

As proof of his brave deed, George cut off the dragon's head and paraded it into town where the people cheered and rejoiced. The citizens of Silene were so grateful to him, and so impressed by his bravery that that very day they were all baptized Christian.

Daniel finished reading and set the book down next to his clock radio. He was surprised to see that it was almost midnight. Along with the howling wind, he could now hear the pitter patter of freezing rain against his bedroom window. Inside, the house was silent.

He leaned back against his pillow, pulled his warm blankets up to his chest, and reflected on the story he'd just read. He thought it was a good book, full of action and excitement, but not very realistic.

Really, it was more like a fairytale than a history book. I wonder if St. George really existed, and if he did, I wonder what he was like. A dragon slayer...that'd be sick...but were there really such things as dragons? I guess it's possible…you never know…. I wonder how he died. The book says that he was a martyr-saint, but the story ended while he was still alive.

Hoping that the book would provide more information, he picked it up and started flipping through its pages.

Just as he'd turned to the table of contents he was startled by a loud *BANG!* outside his window, and the power went out. Other than the glow of his flashlight, he was now in complete darkness.

Hardly daring to breathe, he sat in silence, trying to figure out what had caused the disturbance. He knew that lightning couldn't have struck; it was too early in the season for thunderstorms. Deciding that a tree must have blown down in the storm, he snuggled deeper under his covers, and prepared for sleep. But then he remembered the barn and the newborn foal. He couldn't hear any movement from within the house, so he assumed that the noise hadn't awoken his grandparents. For a moment he considered waking them but in the end decided to go and check on his own first, to see if there was anything to report. If nothing had been damaged he'd go back to bed and tell them about it first thing in the morning.

He climbed out of bed quietly and threw on his jeans and t-shirt. The only sound was that of the wind battering against his bedroom window. Armed with his flashlight, he was about to head for the door when he remembered that he'd left his cross sitting on the bedside table.

He shone his flashlight in that direction. *Yes, it's still there.* He picked it up and slid it on, over his head. The house was dark and quiet, but wearing the cross somehow made him feel more courageous.

He crept down the stairs, threw on his rubber boots and jacket, and headed outdoors.

If he'd hoped to find it brighter outside, he was immediately disappointed. The clouds were heavy and low; darkness was absolute. The snow had turned to sleet, making the ground as slippery as an ice rink, and he repeatedly had to catch his balance to avoid falling. As he walked, slowly and carefully, along the trail toward the barn he wished he'd stayed in the safety and comfort of his warm bed. The sleet beating down on his hood made it hard for him to hear what was going on around him. He kept imagining dark figures lurking behind corners. When he was almost to the barn he stopped and shone his flashlight around, checking to see if everything looked OK.

Several feet away, lying in the middle of the yard was the top half of a pine tree. The force of the wind must have caused it to blow down. Thankfully, it hadn't landed on any buildings. Boughs littered the yard, but he couldn't detect any sign of damage.

He turned and was about to head back toward the house, when he was suddenly overcome with a paralyzing sensation. The rain ceased, and he was engulfed in complete darkness and silence. It felt as though he was being forcefully pulled to the ground by his cross. He fell to his knees. And then, just as suddenly, it stopped.

(V)

He was on his knees breathing hard. With his eyes shut tight he ran both hands along the chain of his pendant trying to figure out what in the world had happened. When he opened them, he was amazed to see that he was no longer on his grandparents' farm but was instead on a winding, country road, and judging by the sun, guessed it must be midday.

A distant drumming sound caught his attention. He stopped and listened as it grew louder. Horses were approaching at a gallop. If he hadn't been in such a state of shock, he would undoubtedly have had the sense to get out of the way but instead remained where he was, kneeling in the centre of the puddle-strewn road, staring around himself in disbelief.

Not far from where he sat, the road disappeared downward into a deep ravine so that the approaching riders had no chance of seeing him until they were almost directly upon him. The man in the lead was the first to react.

"Whoa!" he shouted, pulling back hard on his reigns and throwing his arm into the air signaling the others to a halt.

One of the horses whinnied and reared in protest, and mud splattered in all directions as the startled riders struggled to avoid Daniel's kneeling figure.

For hours, they'd been traveling with no break in the scenery, nothing more to look at than the well-trodden road beneath their feet, rolling mountains on either side, and the unbroken grey sky overhead. The last thing they expected to run into on this quiet stretch of the road was a boy, apparently injured and all alone, so it was with great alarm that they looked down upon his prone figure.

Still frozen to the spot, Daniel stared back at them, awestricken. They were dressed unlike anyone he'd ever seen before.

This can't be happening, he thought, shaking his head and rubbing his eyes with his fists. *I must be dreaming.*

Two of the riders were men, clad in heavy, wool cloaks, long, belted tunics, and leather shoes, and the other was a girl. Daniel thought that she must be about his age, but she looked nothing like any of the girls that he knew. Instead of the usual blue jeans and trendy, designer clothes, she wore a simple, ankle length dress with a long scarf wrapped loosely around her neck and pulled up over her head like a hood. Her bright green eyes peered at him anxiously from behind the security of the men who were now scanning the roadside suspiciously, in search of any hidden danger. One of the horses snorted and stepped backwards nervously.

Was the boy hurt, the men wondered, *or was this a trap?* The countryside was a dangerous place; filthy gangs of bandits, thieves and slave traders were often known to attack unsuspecting travelers.

The man who'd been riding in the lead was the younger of the two. He was in his twenties and had short, black hair, a lean, muscular build, and dark eyes. After muttering something under his breath to the others, he slung the right side of his cloak over his shoulder exposing a beautifully embroidered red tunic and sheathed sword. Looking cautiously from side to side, he began to move toward

Daniel. His expression was intense yet not unkind, and although he said nothing, he rode with such authority that Daniel began to relax. Whatever was going on, surely this man could help.

"Good day," he said. "Are you injured?"

It took Daniel a moment to find his voice. "I...I don't know," he stammered.

The man slid down from his horse and pulled Daniel to his feet. The sudden change of position made Daniel's head spin, and he swayed dangerously on the spot. In an effort to steady himself, he closed his eyes and leaned forward, his hands resting on his knees while he breathed deeply. The air was cool, and he welcomed the smell of mud and grass after so many long, frozen months of winter.

When the feeling had passed he opened his eyes—and gasped. Not only were these strangers dressed oddly but so was he! Instead of his favourite jeans and t-shirt, he was now wearing a brown, hooded wool cloak over a belted tunic, wool leggings, and leather shoes. Quickly he threw his hands to his face, expecting to find that it too had somehow changed.

The stranger watched him curiously. "How did you come to be here, all alone?" he asked. "Is your family nearby?"

"No. I mean, I'm not sure," said Daniel. He looked around, wondering where in the world he was. "Where am I?"

"Bithynia," answered the man.

Daniel toyed with his cross nervously and stared at the ground, wondering where in the world Bithynia was. He had a horrible feeling in the pit of his stomach.

The stranger motioned over his shoulder toward the other man and the young girl, who were still waiting on their horses several feet away. "My comrades and I are on our way to Nicomedia," he said, "the eastern capital of the Roman Empire. Perhaps you've heard of it? 'Tis not far from here."

The Roman Empire, thought Daniel, *of course!*

He'd been studying the history of Europe in class all year. He'd learned about the rise and fall of the Roman Empire as well as of medieval Europe. He knew that, at its height, the Roman Empire had included all of the land surrounding the Mediterranean Sea. It had stretched from England, across Europe, and into Western Asia and North Africa. Many places were named differently then than they are now, which he assumed was why he'd never heard of Bithynia or a city called Nicomedia.

He looked around, hoping to get some kind of a hint as to where he was. Beyond the nearby fields were tree-covered, rolling mountains. Far off in the distance a tall snow capped mountain could be seen.

Think now, he told himself, *where could I be? This man says that Nicomedia is the **eastern** capital of the Roman Empire. I know that Rome, Italy, was always the capital of the west, but that as time wore on, the east became more and more important…more and more wealthy… so that by the late Roman Empire the city of Rome had lost a lot of its power…but where was the capital of the east located? Somewhere in the near east, probably…wait a minute…now I remember! It was in the region where the continents of Europe and Asia collide, in what is now called Turkey, so I must be somewhere in Turkey! But that's insane! I can't possibly be in Turkey during the late Roman Empire! I must be dreaming.*

He rubbed his eyes again.

At this point, the man, who'd been watching him carefully, pulled a waterskin from his pack and offered it to him, motioning for him to take a drink. He was worried.

The boy seemed so confused, and in a few more hours the sun would be setting. Then it would be cold and dark. He decided that they'd have to take him along with them and try and locate his family when they arrived at their destination.

"You're welcome to join us for the remainder of our journey," he said. "When we arrive at Nicomedia we'll help you find your family."

Daniel looked from him to the other two and considered his options. He wasn't in the habit of going off with complete strangers, but under the circumstances, he didn't think that he had any other choice. Until he figured out how he'd come to be in this strange land he doubted if he'd be able to get back home.

He smiled uncertainly. "Sure, if it's no trouble."

The man bowed gracefully and introduced himself. "My name is George."

(VI)

Daniel was in shock.

Could it just be a coincidence, he wondered, *or is this man standing in front of me St. George?*

While he stared open-mouthed, his mind reeling, George turned to the others and introduced them.

"This is my servant, Pasicrates," he said, "and my niece, Perpetua."

They smiled warmly and bowed their heads in greeting. Perpetua bit her tongue. She was curious to learn more about this strange boy. She wondered who he was, and what he was doing here, but like all Christian girls of her era, she'd been taught to exercise humility and modesty in the presence of strangers, which meant keeping her mouth shut and her eyes averted even when it was the last thing she wanted to do.

Pasicrates, on the other hand, felt no need to speak. Unlike Perpetua, he'd long ago perfected the art of patience, an admirable quality in a servant. No one knew his age, but if you'd asked him he would have said that he was older than forty. He was a tall, slim man. The skin around his eyes was lined, and his long dark hair and beard were beginning to go grey.

Daniel bowed self-consciously and introduced himself.

"Come, Daniel," said George, heaving himself back up onto his horse. "We must hurry, or I fear that we will not arrive at Nicomedia before the gate is closed. You can ride with Perpetua."

As Daniel climbed onto the horse, Perpetua caught sight of the cross dangling around his neck. She was intrigued. It was different than any she'd ever seen before, and it looked valuable. Not the sort of thing that most young men would wear, especially while traveling.

Turning to get a better look at it she said, "That's a beautiful pendant. Where did you get it?"

Daniel reached up and wrapped his fingers around it protectively. He still didn't know exactly where he was, or what he was doing here, but he had a feeling that his cross was somehow responsible, which meant that it was very valuable.

"It was a gift," he said vaguely.

"Oh..." said Perpetua,

Daniel avoided her gaze and looked over at George, hoping that she'd lose interest in his cross and turn around. He was confused and wanted to start moving so that he could have time to think.

"It's just that I've never seen a cross quite like that one before," she persisted. "What does it mean?"

He looked at her and frowned. "What does it mean? I don't know...it's a cross....you know...like the one that Jesus died on."

Perpetua gazed wide-eyed at the pendant. "Uncle!" she called. "Daniel is a Christian! Come and see his cross!"

George drew his horse up alongside them and examined Daniel's pendant.

"He wears it in memory of our Lord," said Perpetua.

Daniel couldn't understand why Perpetua was making such a big deal about his cross, but he was even more surprised when George looked into his eyes and said seriously, "These are dangerous times for Christians. Sacred items, such as this, must be well guarded. Keep it close to your heart, brother."

He nodded and tucked it safely under his tunic, wondering what George meant by "dangerous times," but before he could ask, George swung his horse around.

"We have no time to waste," he called over his shoulder. "Let us be off!"

It was a cool day. Low grey clouds hung in the sky. With George in the lead and Pasicrates at the rear, the four travelers rode along in silence. Daniel was so caught up in thought that he was barely aware of his surroundings. Every now and then the trees on either side of them would fall away to reveal fertile fields and orchards, some of which now lay unattended and overgrown with weeds. At one point they saw a young shepherd tending to his flock. Although Daniel was awed by the beauty of the landscape, he was much too overwhelmed to relax and enjoy the ride.

In his head, he went over everything that had happened. He'd been reading a book about St. George, a Roman Christian knight who killed a dragon and died in 303 A.D. Just before midnight, he'd gone outside and suddenly, without warning, been transported back in time to the late Roman Empire. The first person he'd met was a man named George. Daniel was convinced that these were not just coincidences. He remembered the overwhelming sensation of being pulled to the ground by his cross and concluded that somehow it must have magically transported him back in time. And he remembered with apprehension that just before the power had gone out he'd been trying to find out how St. George had died. He glanced around himself nervously, hoping they wouldn't run into a dragon.

His thoughts were interrupted when Perpetua asked, "Where are you from, Daniel?"

He hesitated for a few seconds, unsure of how to answer. Deciding on the truth, he replied, "Canada."

"I've never heard of it," she said. "Is it west of here?"

"Yeah..." he chuckled, "far to the west. Where are you from? Do you live in Nicomedia?"

"I live with my Uncle George now," she said, "but I'm from Palestine. We've been journeying for many days from my homeland."

"Where are your parents?" he asked.

"They died," she said quietly.

Daniel felt terrible. He wished he hadn't asked.

"Sorry," he said awkwardly.

"Oh, please, don't be," she said, smiling confidently. "I know they're in heaven now. They died bravely as Christian martyrs."

Daniel's grandfather had tried to explain to him what this meant, but he still didn't fully understand.

"How?" he asked. "I mean...what happened?"

"Well..." she frowned and closed her eyes, searching for the right words. The wounds left by the memory were still fresh. When she finally opened them again she took a deep breath before beginning. "I suppose it all started with the floods. The rain came with a vengeance...it just rained and rained...so much so, that the river spilled over, causing flooding and devastation to my homeland. Many people lost their homes; some lost their lives." She paused and was quiet for a moment. When she spoke again her tone was bitter. "People began whispering and pointing their fingers at us. They blamed the floods on us Christians. They said that their gods were angry because we refuse to worship them. Eventually the governor had my parents and some others arrested. He tried to force them to offer a sacrifice to the Roman gods, but they wouldn't. They were very brave."

Daniel didn't know what to say. Now he understood what George had meant when he said that these were dangerous times for Christians. The thought of a dragon didn't seem so terrifying anymore. He didn't want to upset Perpetua any more than he already had, but his curiosity prompted him to ask, "How were they killed?"

"They were fed to wild beasts in the stadium."

His stomach lurched, and he was suddenly overcome with an overwhelming sense of fear and panic. He wondered what kind of a place he'd come to where something so barbaric could happen. Their teacher hadn't covered this part of Ancient Rome. Come to think of it, they hadn't discussed religion at all. Fortunately, he was an avid reader. In order to help calm his nerves, he concentrated on trying to remember everything that he knew about religion in the Roman Empire.

He knew that early Romans, like most ancient people, worshiped many gods, such as Zeus, Jupiter, and Mars. Jewish people also lived in Ancient Rome, but unlike their neighbours, they worshiped only one God, the God of the patriarchs, Abraham, Isaac, and Jacob, the same God that Christians and Muslims now worship. But there were no Muslims in Ancient Rome.

Daniel looked around, at the surrounding countryside.

One day this land will be called Turkey, he thought, *and most of the people here will be Muslim, but that won't be for a few hundred more years.* He wondered what year it was. *If it's the year 303, then I'd better watch myself, because that was the year of George's death.*

He leaned over a little to the right, so that he could look past Perpetua, at George. He found it hard to believe that such a young, competent, strong, and healthy man might soon be killed. *Maybe it's a mistake,* he reasoned, *I mean...* he paused to do some quick mental math, *...if it is the year 303, then I've gone back more than 1700 years! Surely the date of his death could be a mistake.* He thought about George's words when he'd seen his cross, *These are dangerous times for Christians...* and he thought about Perpetua's parents, dying in the stadium.

Only three hundred years before now, Jesus was born, and after He died and ascended into heaven, the apostles traveled all around the Empire to spread the message that He was the Messiah. That's how Christianity started, with just a handful of believers, and now it's everywhere. Well, at least, in the twenty first century it's everywhere. Daniel thought about all of the books he'd read about medieval Europe, with kings and queens and knights in shining armour. *They were all Christian too, but now...?*

As they plodded silently along, he stared absent-mindedly at a small white washed hut in the distance with an old mule tied in the yard, and wondered just how many Christians there were in the world in the year 303. *Probably not many if they're being fed to wild beasts.* He shuddered at the thought of it. *But then, how did Christianity spread from a small group of Palestinian Jews to people of all races, all over the globe?* He realized that he'd never really thought about it before.

He was startled out of his reverie when a voice beside him said, "You look like you're deep in thought. Are you thinking about where we might find your parents?" It was George. He'd slowed his pace and was now riding alongside Daniel and Perpetua.

"No," said Daniel. "I was just wondering how many Christians there are in the world now."

"Were you?" said George in surprise. "What an odd thing for you to be thinking about! Well…I don't know how many there are in the world but there are a quite a few in Nicomedia."

"Really?!" exclaimed Daniel. "Even when it's so dangerous?"

"Yes, there are a great number here in the east," George assured him. "Many more than in the west."

"Uncle George knows a lot," bragged Perpetua. "He's traveled to many distant lands. He's a very important commanding officer in the Imperial Army."

"Perpetua," grinned George, "you know I no longer serve in the army. I did though," he explained to Daniel, "for many years. Many of my men were Christian, but now…I don't know…" His voice trailed off and his expression darkened.

"What do you mean you don't know?" asked Daniel.

"Things have changed," said George vaguely.

Daniel stared at him waiting for him to continue, but for several long moments George remained silent, seemingly lost in thought. Finally he looked up into Daniel's eyes and met his gaze. After appearing to reach some sort of a decision, he continued.

"Sometime ago, Emperor Diocletian sent out a command for all soldiers to either offer sacrifices to the Roman gods or be dismissed. I quit. And then I departed on my journey to Palestine to fetch Perpetua. I've been away a longtime…perhaps too long…I fear that things have worsened in my absence. I'm heading back to do what I should have done long ago, to try and talk some sense into the emperor."

"Offer sacrifices!" said Daniel in alarm, his mind filled with disturbing images of young virgins and bubbling volcanoes. "What kind of sacrifices?"

"Incense, of course" said George.

"Oh," said Daniel, breathing a sigh of relief, "incense...of course...well, that's not that big of a deal then, is it?"

Perpetua swung around to face him, her green eyes flashing. "Not a big deal?!" she said indignantly. "But we mustn't! The Lord has forbidden us to worship false gods; it's one of our commandments!"

Daniel was taken aback. "I'm sorry," he said. "I just thought that...you know...under the circumstances...God would understand."

Perpetua glared at him and opened her mouth to speak again but was silenced by a warning look from George, who then turned to Daniel and said calmly, "Being Christian is not always easy, brother, especially in times such as these. 'Tis wrong of Diocletian to put us in such a difficult position, but his threats don't change Gods laws."

Daniel felt his face turn red. He didn't mean to sound like a coward but...fed to wild beasts? It sickened him to think about what Perpetua's parents must have had to endure. *And anyway,* he thought, *what difference does it make if people bow down to other gods? I know that one of the Ten Commandments forbids it, but honestly, does it really matter? I can understand the importance of not killing or stealing and all that, but how does worshipping false gods hurt anyone?*

"I guess I just don't see what the big deal is," he said.

Perpetua scoffed loudly, but he ignored her, adding, "I mean, as long as you're a good person."

"Trust me, Daniel, it matters" said George. "It's the first and most important commandment. 'Love the Lord your

God with your whole heart, your whole soul and your whole mind…and love your neighbour as yourself.' Jesus said so himself."

"But when the punishment is so harsh…?" said Daniel. "I just think that maybe God would understand…under the circumstances."

George smiled doubtfully. "You think so?" he said. "I'm not so certain."

They rode on in silence for a moment, each left to his own thoughts, until George said, "You may be right, Daniel. Who am I to judge? But I can tell you this much: a man may call himself whatever he likes, but it's his actions, not his words, that define who he truly is. As for me, I won't allow my integrity to be compromised by the likes of Diocletian. He can make all the threats he likes, but he can not force me to live a lie."

Daniel marveled at George's bravery. This reminded him of something. "George," he asked, "have you ever killed a dragon?"

The sound of laughter erupted behind Daniel. It was Pasicrates. He'd been so quiet until now that Daniel had almost forgotten he was there.

George looked back at Pasicrates and said with a wide grin, "It's not that funny!"

Eventually Pasicrates stopped laughing enough to speak. "Truly, now I've heard everything!" he said, still chuckling and wiping tears from his eyes.

Daniel was embarrassed. "Are there no such things as dragons then?" he asked.

"Oh, there may be dragons," said George, "I've just never met one." Still grinning, he called out over his shoulder. "And I'll remember to thank God in my evening prayers, for Pasicrates obviously thinks I'd fare poorly in an encounter with one."

"My prayers will be devoted to you and your safety, my lord," there was no humour in Pasicrates tone now. "For if you go through with your plans tomorrow, you shall face an evil dragon named Galerius, and for this you shall need the help of all the heavenly angels."

Daniel wondered about these words but decided that now was not the time to ask. He'd wait until he and Perpetua were alone.

+

He didn't have to wait long. Soon George said, "Perpetua, you and Daniel can ride on ahead if you like. Around the next bend you'll find a stream. We'll be stopping there for a few moments, to let the horses drink."

When he and Perpetua reached the spot, they dismounted and led their horse to the water.

Daniel stretched his legs and walked along the edge of the stream, picking up rocks as he went and tossing them in. Further along, he noticed a trail, which disappeared through a gap in the trees. Looking back he saw that Perpetua was busy tying her horse to a tree. He hesitated a moment and then quickly sped off down the trail. If he hurried he'd be back before anyone noticed he was gone.

For several feet the trail led him through a tangle of trees and shrubs. When he emerged on the other side he gasped. He was standing on the edge of a cliff overlooking the sea. Several miles to the east, the ancient city of Nicomedia rose up majestically from the banks of a busy harbour.

In the early fourth century this booming metropolis was an important trading centre and home to the most powerful man in the Roman Empire, Emperor Diocletian. Daniel gazed in awe at the emperor's palace and the surrounding white buildings which lay sprawled out along the edge of the sea. The harbour was bustling with activity; slaves worked tirelessly loading cargo onto a ship while fishing vessels unloaded their catch of the day. Many other vessels could be seen gently bobbing in the waves offshore.

Encircling the city like a protective snake was a great, stone wall. Daniel remembered the city in the legend of St. George; it also had a wall surrounding it.

Could the story be true? he wondered. *Could this be the place?*

As he stood, gazing out over the sea, he heard a rustling noise in the bushes behind him. Nervously, he turned to look.

"BOO!" A figure burst from the trees.

Instinctively, he jumped and staggered backwards, his hands shielding his face from danger. When he regained his senses Perpetua was standing over him, laughing hysterically.

"Very funny," said Daniel sarcastically.

Still giggling, Perpetua approached him and stood by his side. "Wow!" she breathed when she caught sight of the view. "That must be Nicomedia. I imagine we'll be there before too long."

Daniel's thoughts returned to fortified walls...and dragons. "Perpetua," he asked, "what did Pasicrates mean when he said that tomorrow George would be facing a dragon named Galerius?"

Perpetua looked at Daniel and smirked. "Wherever you're from must be a very long way from here," she said. "Galerius is our caesar."

When Daniel continued to look confused, she added, "The most powerful man in the Eastern Empire, second only to our emperor, Diocletian."

"Oh," said Daniel, "you mean like a second in command?"

Perpetua nodded. "And he hates Christians. This is why Pasicrates calls him a dragon." She glanced over her shoulder before adding in a hushed voice, "Before we left Palestine I overheard my Uncle George talking with some of the other adults. They told him that Galerius has spent most of this winter in meetings with our emperor. They fear that he's been trying to convince Diocletian to start a great persecution against the Christians. Galerius would like to see us all dead. He's a wicked, arrogant man. He thinks he's a god, and he believes that we should all be punished for refusing to worship him."

Daniel wasn't surprised. He remembered reading that in Ancient Rome emperors were often worshipped like gods.

"Perpetua…Daniel!" George was calling them.

Before Perpetua could reply, Daniel pulled her aside and whispered urgently, "This might sound like a strange question, but I really need to know…What year is it?"

Perpetua gave him a sympathetic look. "You must have suffered quite a blow," she said. "Did you fall from your horse?"

Daniel shrugged. He wasn't about to tell her the truth. She'd never believe him anyway.

"It's the Three Hundred and Third Year of Our Lord," she said.

Daniel's stomach dropped. So it was true. 303 A.D. Despite having suspected it all along, he looked around himself, stunned, wondering how on earth he'd ended up in the early fourth century and how he would ever find his way home.

While Perpetua hollered their whereabouts to George, Daniel pulled his cross out of his tunic and clenched it in his fist, telling himself that he must never lose it, that for some strange reason it had brought him to this foreign place and that surely one day it would send him back home. He hoped.

George emerged from the trees, followed closely by Pasicrates.

"Spectacular view!" said George as he approached the bank and gazed out toward the sea.

A second later Pasicrates gasped and, pointing toward Nicomedia, cried, "Look! The cathedral! It's been destroyed!"

The cathedral that had once stood proudly on a hilltop overlooking the city now lay in ruin. Early that morning, before dawn, the emperor's soldiers had forced open the doors and destroyed all of its contents. The books of the Holy Scriptures were burned, sacred instruments smashed. Nothing remained intact. Under order of the emperor, the soldiers had used axes and other iron tools to tear the cathedral to the ground. After several hours all that remained was a pile of rubble.

As Daniel and the others looked on in horror from their seaside vantage point, they could see soldiers still milling about at the scene.

"It's as we'd feared," said George through gritted teeth. "I only pray that Bishop Anthimus has managed to save some of our sacred writings, and that our brothers and sisters are all safe."

"Amen," said Pasicrates solemnly.

Hoping for the best but expecting the worst, the four of them hurried off in the direction of Nicomedia.

(VII)

As they approached the city the road widened and became busier. Daniel was amazed to see so many people traveling in the direction of Nicomedia. When he questioned Perpetua she explained that the following day was the Festival of Terminalia and that many people would be gathering in the city to enjoy the ceremonies. He learned that this holiday was celebrated once a year, in honour of Terminus, the god of boundaries. A shiver ran down his spine, and he wondered darkly whether the destruction of the cathedral on such a day was mere coincidence or whether the emperor was calling on the god Terminus to help put an end to Christianity.

While they hurried along he tried to take in as much as he could of the people they passed. Most traveled on foot but some rode in horse-drawn wooden wagons loaded with produce, like oranges and figs, and once they passed an old woman leading a mule that was burdened down with beautiful, brightly woven garments. He supposed they were on their way to sell their wares at the market.

After a time, looming ahead in the distance he could see Nicomedia's great, stone wall and a large arched opening which he assumed was the entrance to the city. Standing on each side of the entrance were two armed Roman soldiers.

The closer they got the more nervous he became. Staring at that wall brought to his mind other, more infamous walls, like the Berlin Wall, and the Bethlehem Wall. He was uncomfortably reminded that walls often serve a dual purpose — to keep out the enemy as well as to keep in the inhabitants. He felt for his cross and tucked it safely under his tunic.

At that moment George looked back at him and caught his eye. Sensing their fear, he smiled reassuringly and slowed his horse to allow Daniel and Perpetua a chance to draw up alongside him.

"Have no fear, everything will work out," he said soothingly. "When we pass through the gate I want you to stay close to me and don't say a word. As soon as we enter the city we'll go to the home of a good friend of mine. That's where we'll stay tonight. He's a deacon*," he said to Daniel, "and he may know where we can find your parents." He paused before asking, "Do you remember anything more?"

Daniel felt terrible having to lie to George. For a brief moment he contemplated telling him the truth but, realizing how ridiculous it would sound, instead replied, "No, nothing."

"Well, cheer up," said George. "I'm sure we'll find them." Before moving ahead he reminded them, once more, to remain silent and keep close.

When they reached the entrance the road narrowed and they fell in line, single file, amid the other weary travelers. Looking up at the wall, Daniel was horrified to see a grossly decaying human head hanging on display. The features were hard to make out and flies were buzzing noisily around the long matted hair which was caked in dried

---

* Deacons are members of the clergy who serve as assistants to priests and bishops.

blood. He shuddered as they passed, wondering what sort of crime the victim had committed in order to receive such a brutal punishment.

Slowly they filed past the armed soldiers. Daniel peered at them through the corner of his eye. There were two stationed on either side. They had a bored and arrogant look about them. He was reminded of his pet cat while it sat sunning with its eyes half closed and tail twitching. He knew better than to provoke these men. Their uniforms consisted of red tunics worn under shiny, scaled armour that covered their shoulders and torso, metal helmets designed to come low over their ears and topped with a bright red crest made of horse hair, leather boots, and, Daniel noticed with unease, deadly swords which hung from their hips on belted sheaths. For warmth, they wore heavy, blood red cloaks, tied, not in front, but above the right shoulder to allow their sword arm unobstructed movement.

One of the soldiers nodded to George and Pasicrates as they passed but said nothing. Daniel put his hands around Perpetua's trembling waist and gave her a comforting squeeze. Once inside the gate he relaxed a little and looked around in wonder.

After the peace and quiet of the countryside, the noise and chaos of the ancient city was a feast to the senses. Never before had he seen such squalor, nor such splendour. Majestic, marble buildings and monuments towered alongside long rows of ramshackle, dingy shops. The narrow streets were buzzing with men and women hurrying about their daily routines. Most were dressed, like Pasicrates, in simple tunics, but others wore long, colourful garments of silk and linen, finely woven scarves, and funny shaped hats or turbans. Children in filthy, threadbare rags played noisily in the streets, chasing one another past busy merchants and donkeys burdened down by heavy loads.

The city was alive and signs of new growth were everywhere. Half-constructed buildings dotted the skyline, and the familiar sounds of hammers pounding on metal filled the air. Nicomedia was a prosperous centre of commerce and trade and a true mosaic of people and culture. As they wound their way through the crowds, Daniel overheard bits and pieces of conversations spoken in foreign languages and wished, more than once, that they weren't in such a rush; there was so much to see!

They rode their horses to a large stable located on the edge of the city. Daniel waited impatiently while the others gathered their belongings and made sure that the horses were attended to.

Finally they set off again, this time on foot. The paved roads were muddy in places and littered with filth. Daniel did his best to step around the puddles and the muck. A couple of mangy dogs wandered by, their noses hovering close to the ground, in search of their next meal.

After several minutes they came to a large, square, open area surrounded by magnificent buildings and dotted with statues of emperors. This was the forum, the heart of the city, where people did their shopping and banking and where they came to listen to public speakers deliver the news.

At the entrance stood a tall, white column, topped with a large and impressive statue of Emperor Diocletian. Next to it, an old, and desperately thin, blind man sat cross-legged in the dirt, begging for handouts. George stopped long enough to drop several coins into his cup* before moving on.

The forum was always a busy place, particularly on holidays. Daniel struggled to keep up as he gazed around curiously at the variety of goods being bought, sold, and traded. There were stalls scattered about, selling such things as jewelry, woven rugs, fresh produce, and live poultry. It was already late in the day, the sun was low in the sky, and the festivities were beginning to get underway. Over the noise of the crowd, Daniel thought that he could hear music playing somewhere in the distance. Gradually it grew louder, until they came upon a teenaged boy playing a cheerful tune on a flute next to a warm, blazing fire. He had dark skin and wore his hair in long, matted dreadlocks. A large group had begun to gather around him, some dancing and laughing and carrying on, while others enjoyed food and wine they'd purchased from the vendors. Daniel stared at them as he walked past, until one of the men caught his eye and threw him a toothless grin. Quickly, he looked away, focusing instead on a white temple towering nearby, dedicated to an unfamiliar Roman god.

He followed his companions through the forum, without stopping. They continued for sometime along narrow streets lined with shops. Most of the shopkeepers were busy closing up for the day. The further they traveled from the forum the quieter the streets became. He was

---

* Almsgiving (donating to the poor) began with Christianity. Prior to that, wealthy people would help fund public events out of a sense of civic responsibility and with the expectation that their donation would bring them public recognition and advantage. Jesus introduced a new way of thinking when he said to give to the poor in secret, out of love and charity.

astonished when they came upon a group of slaves carrying two long, horizontal poles on which sat an elaborately decorated, enormous box. It had beautiful silk curtains hanging on each side. As they hurried past, a dark, bearded man in a turban pushed the curtain aside to peer out.

Daniel's feet were beginning to ache when they finally veered off the road and headed toward a large and rather shabby looking tenement block. They entered through a doorway which led into an open courtyard, climbed three flights of rickety, wooden stairs, continued down a long hall, and finally stopped in front of a door on which was drawn one of the earliest Christian symbols.

(VIII)

George knocked, and they waited for what seemed to be an eternity.

The hall smelled strongly of wood smoke and food cooking. Noises floated in the air, merging and then separating...a baby crying...a man coughing...dishes clattering...laughter...voices...

Finally the door creaked and slowly opened to reveal a man in his late twenties with unruly black hair. At the sight of them his face lit up.

"George! Pasicrates! You've returned!"

After gripping them both in a tight hug and kissing them on each cheek, the man glanced nervously down the hallway and urged them inside.

Daniel was thankful to enter the warmth and safety of the apartment. While the men were reacquainted, he stood quietly to one side and looked around.

The room was small and sparsely furnished but clean and tidy. Against the far wall on a wooden side table, three candles burned dimly beneath a large, crude painting of a shepherd holding a lamb. Other than this, the walls were completely bare. Daniel knew that the shepherd in the painting represented Jesus. He'd seen one similar to it before, though much smaller, at his grandparent's house, stuck to the fridge amid an assortment of photos of grandchildren and inspirational magnets.

He was startled when a door on the other side of the room swung open and a young woman with long brown hair and olive skin appeared in the doorway. Her face shone in the warm glow of a small clay lamp, which she held in her outstretched hand. She wore a tense, frightened expression, but when she spotted George and Pasicrates her shoulders relaxed and she smiled and rushed across the room to greet them.

"Juliana," exclaimed George in delight, "it's good to see you again, sister." He drew her into a warm embrace and kissed her on each cheek. "How have you been?"

She choked back tears and shook her head, too emotional to speak.

"These are difficult times," said George soothingly, "we mustn't lose faith."

"Yes," she nodded, wiping away her tears and forcing a smile, "yes, of course…thank God you're alive…and you're here." Her voice broke as she struggled to contain a fresh wave of tears.

George drew her into a comforting hug.

As soon as she'd regained her composure she turned her attention to Pasicrates, who was standing with his back to her so absorbed in conversation with Deacon Adrian that he hadn't noticed her arrival. Tentatively, she reached out and touched his arm. When he turned and saw her standing there his furrowed brows were instantly wiped away and replaced with a broad smile.

"Juliana," he said cheerfully. "God bless you, sister!"

While they exchanged greetings George walked over to the corner where Perpetua and Daniel stood waiting.

He smiled and winked encouragingly before clearing his throat to get everyone's attention.

"Daniel...Perpetua," he said, "these are my good friends, Deacon Adrian, and his wife*, Juliana."

Perpetua moved forward gracefully and kneeled before Deacon Adrian. "Your blessing, Father Deacon," she said.

Daniel watched in uncomfortable silence as Deacon Adrian stretched out his hand and bestowed a blessing upon her. He dreaded the moment when the blessing would end, when all eyes would inevitably turn in his direction. He had no idea what he was expected to say, or do. He wished they could just shake hands or, even better, that he could just disappear.

Finally the blessing ended and Deacon Adrian turned toward him. "Daniel is it?" he asked.

Daniel nodded shyly but said nothing. He felt stupid, totally out of his element. Hoping that George would rescue him he looked up at him imploringly.

George grinned good-naturedly and took a step forward. "Daniel is from Canada," he explained, "somewhere west of here."

"Canada?" repeated Deacon Adrian. "I've not heard of it."

Daniel thought that he detected a hint of suspicion in his voice. In a determined effort to avoid eye contact, he

---

* During the first few centuries, there was no formal rule prohibiting the clergy from marrying but it was considered problematic and most chose not to. By the end of the first millennium corruption had become a problem and marriage had become more common. Some clergy were leaving Church property to their family in their will. This caused the Church to introduce reform and to finally impose the rule of celibacy at the Second Lateran Council of 1139.

stared down at his feet, his heart pounding so hard he was sure everyone in the room could hear it.

"Nor have I," said George, with not the least bit of concern, "but we discovered him on the road west of the city, kneeling in the dirt, apparently injured and all alone, with no manner of transport save his feet. I don't know where Canada is, but I doubt very much that he traveled all the way to Bithynia on foot. Unfortunately, he can't remember a thing. He's no idea of the whereabouts of his family."

Hearing it told in this manner made Daniel realize just how strange and unbelievable his situation must appear to others, and he was suddenly overcome with a deep sense of gratitude and loyalty toward George for his unquestioning kindness.

Deacon Adrian smirked at George and shook his head in mild disbelief. "So you invited him to join you? How very like you, George," he teased. "You persistently turn away every offer of marriage, claiming that you're too busy or some such nonsense, yet you always seem to have time to rescue orphans."

"What would you have had me do?" cut in George defensively. "Leave him there? And would you please not start on me again," he scowled. "You know as well as I do that I'm in no position to take a wife. The life of a soldier is, in my mind anyway, hardly conducive to marriage."

"The life of a soldier, yes," agreed Deacon Adrian with a wry smile, "but…are you still a soldier?"

George opened his mouth to speak but closed it again, clearly at a loss for words. He'd always been a soldier, but now? He stared at Deacon Adrian in brooding silence. Soldier or not, he was still in no position to take a wife, not while his future remained so uncertain. For months now he'd felt as though he was standing at a crossroads, not just him, but everyone, the entire Empire, and that something monumental was about to happen, but what?

Aware that every eye in the room was fixed on him, he pushed these unpleasant thoughts to the back of his mind and forced a smile. "You really are relentless, you know that?"

Deacon Adrian laughed out loud and patted him on the back. "I just want what's best for you, brother," he said sincerely.

"Don't worry about me," said George. "There are plenty of other things to worry about, like widows and orphans, for instance." He waved his hand in Daniel's direction, steering the conversation back to the matter at hand. "Daniel's a brother," he said. "He remembers that much. I was hoping that you might have heard some news among our brethren?"

At the mention of "brethren," Deacon Adrian's smile faded, and his face clouded over.

"No," he said, shaking his head. "No, I'm afraid not. But lately our people are frightened and a little more guarded than usual...and now with the cathedral destroyed..." He shrugged his shoulders helplessly.

"Well, no matter," said George, smiling bravely and squeezing Daniel's shoulder reassuringly, "we'll ask around."

"And we'll include you in our prayers," added Juliana sincerely.

"Yes," muttered Deacon Adrian bitterly, "we'll add you to our litany."

Juliana threw him a reproachful look. "How are you feeling now?" she asked, in a tactful attempt to wipe away her husband's morose words. "Are you injured?"

Daniel shook his head. "No," he said, "no, I'm fine." All this attention was making him feel guilty. He considered telling them the truth. With a faint flicker of hope he thought, *Maybe they can help me find my way back to my grandparents.* He was about to speak when a bell suddenly began to toll loudly.

DING! DONG! DING! DONG!

He looked at Perpetua questioningly.

"'Tis the end of the day," she whispered in his ear. "The gate to the city is closing."

The adults turned and moved into the other room. The moment was lost. Although Daniel knew that he was among friends he had never felt so alone.

(IX)

Daniel followed the others into the living room where two grey-haired men were sitting, engrossed in quiet conversation. One of them was Bishop Anthimus, and the other Lactantius. They had been discussing the day's events, but when they caught sight of George and the others they stopped talking mid-sentence and rose to their feet.

George and Pasicrates crossed the room and bowed in greeting, asking the bishop to bestow a blessing upon them.

"May the Lord bless you, my children," he said, and embraced them both, as a father would his sons after a long separation. "Surely this is some sort of a miracle," he said to George, "that after all of these months you would return on the very day that our cathedral is destroyed."

"I disagree," said George. "A miracle would have been for me to arrive sooner and to have prevented this heinous crime."

The bishop shrugged and, placing his right hand on George's shoulder, said wisely, "We must have faith, my son, and remember that our way is not always the Lord's way." While he turned to reseat himself he motioned toward the doorway to where Daniel and Perpetua were waiting shyly.

"And who have we here?" he asked.

George waved the two of them over. "Bishop…Lactantius… this is Perpetua and Daniel."

Daniel bowed politely as he'd seen the others do. He expected Perpetua to do the same, but instead, she fell to her knees at the bishop's feet, buried her face in her hands, and started crying. Daniel wondered what was going on. He looked around the room at the others hoping to find some sort of an explanation, but they were all staring sadly at her.

Bishop Anthimus laid his hands gently on her head. "May God bless you, child," he murmured. "You mustn't cry. Have faith, and look forward to the day when you'll be reunited with your parents in our Father's heavenly kingdom."

It had been a long day. Daniel had been so busy worrying about his own problems that he'd forgotten about Perpetua's recent loss.

Juliana entered the room with a platter of food. After setting it on the table, she gathered Perpetua in her arms and led her to a corner where a large, woven rug was laid. She motioned for Daniel to come and join them.

"The two of you must be exhausted," she said quietly. "Sit here and relax. Help yourselves to some food, and I'll be back in a few minutes with some drinks."

At the mention of food Daniel realized how hungry he was. *No wonder I'm starving*, he thought as he approached the platter, *it's been more than seventeen hundred years since my last meal.*

The men were seated on the other side of the room, deep in discussion. He reached the table first, and stared down at the simple meal, wondering where to begin. Spread out neatly on a round, wooden platter were several large pieces of flat bread stuffed with cheese, surrounded by dried apricots and figs.

He looked up when Perpetua approached the table, her eyes red and puffy. "Are you all right?" he asked.

She smiled feebly and nodded. After choosing a piece of bread, she returned to her place in the corner.

Daniel loaded up his plate with food and was about to start shoveling it down when he noticed Perpetua kneeling serenely in prayer. Her eyes were closed, and her bread was sitting untouched on the plate in front of her. Suddenly, he felt awkward.

Kneeling next to her, he set down his plate and closed his eyes. After a minute or so, he opened them slightly but closed them right away when he saw that she was still praying. He wondered how long this would take; his stomach was grumbling. He tried to think of a prayer.

God, thank you for this food. Protect me from all danger and please, help me to find my way home.

When he finished, he snuck another peek at Perpetua. This time, to his delight, she was eating. Without hesitation, he broke off a piece of the bread and ate it.

While he sat cross-legged, enjoying his meal, he gazed around the room in an attempt to learn a little more about his hosts and their lifestyle. There didn't appear to be an indoor bathroom nor, in fact, any type of indoor plumbing or running water. He remembered that the Romans had public baths and toilets. He couldn't see a garbage can anywhere and decided that even if he were able to find one, it would probably be pretty empty. He suspected that these people weren't very wasteful. There was no evidence anywhere of discarded wrappings or packaging. He remembered that plastic hadn't even been invented yet, nor had the printing press. The latter explained the lack of books. At home there were books and magazines everywhere, on shelves, end tables, next to the toilet, but prior to the fifteenth century when the printing press was invented, all books were handwritten and so were very rare and valuable. This meant that other than the wealthy and ruling classes, most people were illiterate. But bishops, priests, and deacons could all read, they had to, it was part of their job. While he ate the rest of his bread, Daniel scanned the room for any evidence of scrolls or books.

His ears perked up when he heard George ask, "And what happened to the sacred scriptures? Were you able to save any from being burned?"

"Yes," said Bishop Anthimus, "yesterday evening we retrieved the most valuable and hid them here. Sadly, we were forced to leave many behind. We couldn't take them all; it would have looked suspicious. We owe what we have to the bravery of one of our sisters who works as a servant within the palace. Several days ago she overheard the emperor discussing his plans to destroy the cathedral and set fire to all of our sacred writings. She managed to get word to Lactantius in time for him to forewarn us."

"What happened to the Gospel of Thomas?" George asked anxiously. "Was it saved?"

"I'm afraid not," the bishop sighed, and shook his head. "We couldn't take them all, George. I'm sorry, but it was among the ones left behind. Difficult decisions had to be made. I've been in communication with some of the other bishops over these past few months. As you know, we've been worried for some time now that something like this could happen. There have been many disagreements over which Scriptures should be protected above all, but most of my brethren believe that the Gospels of Matthew, Mark, Luke, and John are of the utmost importance...as well, of course, as any writings by the apostle Paul. These were rescued, among others."

While he spoke, Juliana poured each of the men a cup of wine. As she picked up the empty tray and was preparing to leave, she said, "Wouldn't it be better if our Scriptures were gathered together and bound in one holy book? It would make things so much less confusing."

"Ridiculous!" scoffed Lactantius.

"I agree with Juliana," said George.

"As do I," agreed the bishop, nodding. "If the Church wishes to survive, we must set aside our differences and focus on unity. One holy book would help us to achieve this goal."

"It's unlikely to happen," argued Lactantius, "and I'll tell you why. Our bishops would never agree on which Scriptures to include."*

Daniel found this conversation fascinating. He hadn't realized that throughout the early Christian era there had been no Bible. That instead, various sacred writings had floated loosely around the empire as independent books. And he was really surprised to hear them talk about disagreements in the Church. He'd assumed that, prior to the Protestant Reformation in the sixteenth century, Christians had always worshipped uniformly, as one, under the Catholic Church.** Evidently he was wrong.

---

* Jesus and his apostles never left us a defined set of religious books. As a result, during the first few centuries, writings attributed to various apostles circulated around the Empire. Some of these books were legitimate and some were frauds. The Fathers of the Church had to determine which books were legitimate (actually written by the early apostles) before they could canonize (make official) the books of the Bible.

** *Catholic* is the Latin term for *universal*. As Christianity spread and Jesus's teachings were written down, arguments and power struggles arose. The early Church fathers sought unity in the hopes that Christians all over the world would worship together as one universal Church.

His attention was diverted when Juliana crouched down next to him and offered him a drink. He took the cup and drank from it. It was wine mixed with water. For the first time in hours, he relaxed; his meal had left him full and satisfied. He glanced over at Perpetua and was not surprised to find that she'd fallen fast asleep. After reaching for a nearby blanket and throwing it gently over her, he turned his attention back to the others.

Lactantius appeared agitated. He paced back and forth while he spoke. "The early apostles left us a written record of the life and teachings of our Lord Jesus Christ so that we might learn the way to salvation. If the soldiers succeed in burning all of our Gospels this knowledge will be lost...forever!" He stopped and stared at those seated around him, his eyes wide with fear. "Without God's Word, the Church will most assuredly die," he whispered, "a slow death...by starvation!"

Daniel shivered involuntarily and pulled a blanket up around himself.

"The emperor is no fool," continued Lactantius, once again pacing the floor, "he knows exactly what he is doing."

"My dear Lactantius," said Bishop Anthimus calmly, "have you no faith? Do you honestly believe that Emperor Diocletian is more powerful than God?"

"I'm afraid, Bishop," whispered Lactantius urgently, "that the destruction of the cathedral is only the beginning. I fear that a widespread persecution of the divine religion is at hand. What Emperor Diocletian and Galerius Caesar want, more than anything, is to purge the Empire, and in fact the world, of Christianity."

Everyone sat in silence for a while, digesting the full meaning of these ominous words.

George was the first to speak. "Bishop, I think it would be best for you to leave Nicomedia at once and take as many of our sacred writings with you as possible."

"I agree," said Deacon Adrian. "Lactantius is right. I too have heard evil rumours of a great persecution. You must escape to the wilderness."

"You would have me abandon my flock when they need me most?" said Bishop Anthimus, incredulously. He shook his head stubbornly. "No, I can't leave. I've taken a sacred oath to serve my children, even in times of danger. I won't break my vow."

"We're not suggesting that you abandon us, only that you escape to someplace safe for the time being and take our Holy Scriptures with you," reasoned George. He paused before adding, "I think we all agree that protecting our Scriptures is of the utmost importance. If Lactantius and Deacon Adrian are right, then it is only a matter of time before the soldiers discover where we've hidden them."

Lactantius resumed his seat next to the bishop. "I think you should listen to George," he pleaded. "What good will you be to your flock if the emperor has you imprisoned? If you escape to the safety of a neighbouring village, you can continue to preach and to encourage us in the form of letters*."

Bishop Anthimus looked from one to the other of his friends. He was a man of faith; he trusted in God completely. He had no fear of the Roman authorities. But when he considered the difficult times that lay in store for his people, he was overcome with sadness and loving compassion. He

---

* It was common practice for bishops to send letters to the Christians in their diocese as a means of preaching and settling disagreements. The New Testament contains a number of such letters.

was torn between his loyalty to his friends and his responsibility to the common good. The burden of protecting the Holy Scriptures for the benefit of future generations weighed heavily on him.

"I'll think about it," he said finally, "but not tonight." He rose from his chair. "Tonight I must serve the Lord by leading my people in prayer. Father Paul has spent the day preparing a place of worship for us. There's an old temple on the edge of the city which was recently consecrated to the Lord. It's not very large, but, under the circumstances, it will do. I hope to see most of you at the vigil. We must come together and pray for our emperor."

As a show of respect, the others all rose from their seats to bid him farewell.

"We'll be joining you shortly, Bishop," said George. "Do you expect many others to attend?"

Bishop Anthimus shrugged his shoulders. "Truly, I don't know," he sighed. "I suspect that many people will be too frightened to—" He stopped mid-sentence and listened.

Someone was pounding on the front door.

(X)

Daniel was startled by a loud knock at the door.

The noise awoke Perpetua from her sleep, and she scrambled to her knees. George quickly stretched his arm out toward her, motioning for her to remain still.

The room was completely silent as they all waited to hear what would happen next.

Knock! Knock! Knock! Knock!

Juliana scurried in quietly from the front room with a look of apprehension on her face. "Who can it be at this hour?" she whispered to Deacon Adrian.

He put his arm around her protectively and looked inquiringly toward George who nodded before heading toward the door. Deacon Adrian followed.

The others waited anxiously, listening for any sign of danger.

Daniel couldn't stand the suspense. He tiptoed quietly and peeked around the corner into the other room.

Deacon Adrian and George stood side by side with the door open wide. Darkness was falling quickly. In the fading light of the setting sun Daniel could make out a figure standing alone in the doorway.

"What do you see?" whispered Perpetua.

"Someone wearing a long, hooded cloak" said Daniel. "I can't see his face."

"Is he alone?" asked Lactantius anxiously.

Daniel nodded.

Just then, the visitor pulled back his hood to reveal his face. He appeared to be around the same age as George and was stocky, with short, brown hair, a broad nose and a cleft chin. At the sight of him, Deacon Adrian bowed low and George drew him into a welcoming hug.

"He's a friend," said Daniel in a low voice.

They all breathed a sigh of relief.

As George turned to lead their guest in out of the dark, Daniel quickly hurried back to his seat next to Perpetua.

The sound of muffled voices and footsteps followed.

Before long, the three men stepped into the room. Deacon Adrian was the first to enter. He shot a meaningful look in the direction of Bishop Anthimus and Lactantius before stepping aside and announcing, "Please welcome Flavius Valerius Constantine."

Everyone bowed deeply. Perpetua, who had remained on her knees, now stretched out her arms and bowed so low that her long dark hair sprawled out on the floor in front of her. Daniel wondered who this stranger was. One thing was clear; he was obviously a man of importance. Although he was young, he stood tall and oozed confidence as he nodded politely to each of them.

When he spotted Lactantius, he faltered. He had hoped to sneak in and out of the city quickly, without being seen by anyone from the palace. "Greetings, Lactantius," he stammered.

"Peace be with you, my Lord," answered Lactantius. "It's been awhile since we last met. What brings you to Nicomedia?"

Constantine hesitated. He knew that it was dangerous for him to be here, among Christians. If Galerius found out, he'd accuse him of treason and have him killed at once. While Galerius was caesar in the East, Constantine's father, Constantius, was caesar in the West. Constantine was an ambitious young man who showed every sign of following in his father's footsteps, and in Ancient Rome this kind of ambition could earn a person some very mortal enemies. Constantine did not wish to give Galerius an excuse to have him killed, but when news had reached him that George was on his way to Nicomedia, he'd felt that he owed it to his friend to warn him of the dangers that he would soon be facing. After all, George had bravely put his life on the line for him, countless times, while they'd battled side by side.

"I won't be staying," he explained. "I've come to speak to George."

His initial fear at seeing someone he recognized was soon surpassed by curiosity. He wondered why Lactantius was here. Surely, he too was aware of the risks involved. Although Constantine didn't know him well, he'd always admired the old man's intellect. On a couple of occasions he'd had the opportunity to sit with him in the palace gardens and discuss history and philosophy. Just recently, he'd heard a rumour that Lactantius was no longer living at the palace. Meeting him here seemed to confirm this. Anxious to know more, he asked, "Word has it that you've resigned from your job as Diocletian's Official Professor of Rhetoric.* Is this true?"

---

* Prior to his conversion, Lactantius served as an advisor to Emperor Diocletian, preparing speeches and letters etc. Often described as the Christian Cicero, he is famous for writing Christian apologetics (arguments in defense of Christianity).

"Yes, it's true," answered Lactantius. "I really had no choice though...the emperor has become increasingly paranoid of Christians these past few months...quite hostile really, and...oh," he paused, "but you may not have heard! I'm a Christian now."

"No," said Constantine, "I hadn't heard." He wasn't surprised though. "What will you do now?" he asked. "Where will you live?"

"I'm renting a small flat not far from here," said Lactantius. "I plan to start selling my writings in order to eke out a living."

Constantine glanced around himself at the blank walls and sparse furnishings. He wondered why anyone would choose to leave the luxurious comfort of the palace for such poverty. He studied the old man for several moments before asking, "And have you any regrets?"

Lactantius laughed. "Regrets? Oh my dear boy, no. I'm an old man. I've spent my entire life searching for meaning, for happiness, for inner peace, so many years wasted" he sighed, "*that* perhaps is my only regret—that I didn't discover the one, true God sooner."

Constantine had heard it all before. He knew many people who had switched over to the new religion, the one they called The Way. Personally, he didn't know what to think. Like most Romans, he'd always been taught to fear and respect the gods because they were believed to be the source of Rome's power. It was really no wonder that Diocletian was so worried about the spread of Christianity. From his perspective the popularity of this new religion spelled certain doom for the Empire, but Constantine wasn't so sure anymore, maybe the Christians were right, maybe theirs was a more powerful God. These were times of uncertainty and instability. The tribes to the north and east were restless. The Empire was crumbling. Change was in the air, and at times the tension was so thick that Constantine could almost taste it. He knew what lay in store for the Christians, and it gave him an uneasy feeling.

Turning abruptly to George, he said, "I must speak to you in private."

+

Daniel sat with his back against the wall, drumming his fingers impatiently on the floor. He wished he had something to do.

Shortly after Constantine's arrival, Perpetua had been called into the kitchen to help Juliana tidy up. Daniel had carried in a few dishes in an effort to help out but had soon been shooed from the room. Before leaving, he'd seen enough to know that kitchens in Ancient Rome were nothing like the ones at home. There was no fridge, stove, or dishwasher, not even a sink! Instead, a circular basin of water sat upon a long wooden shelf that ran the entire length of the room. Other shelves were stacked with dishes, pots, water jugs, herbs, and an assortment of dried foods.

The door swung open, and Perpetua walked past him, a pitcher of dirty water balancing on her hip. Carefully she hoisted it onto the window ledge and dumped its contents onto the street below. He remembered reading somewhere that before indoor plumbing, people would often dump their chamber pots out of open windows. He grimaced at the thought of it and made a mental note to never walk directly under an open window.

"What are you doing now?" he asked as she headed back toward the kitchen. He was hoping she'd be done soon and would join him.

"Cleaning," she blushed ashamedly. "Juliana doesn't have any servants. I don't mind though," she added hurriedly. "Mother always encouraged me to be helpful, and anyway, it's awfully nice of them to have us. Don't you agree?"

"Huh? Oh...yeah," he nodded as he watched her leave. "Yeah, it sure is." For the first time, he wondered just how long he'd be staying. Obviously George and Deacon Adrian wouldn't have any luck tracking down his "missing" parents. And then what? Would he be forced to live here the rest of his life? He wished he could figure out exactly how he got here and some way to get home. He felt totally useless just sitting, doing nothing. The others were all busy. Soon after Constantine arrived, Pasicrates had disappeared into a back room to reorganize the travel packs, and Lactantius and Deacon Adrian had left for the temple. He'd wanted to go with them, but they'd forbidden it. They'd advised him to try and get some sleep. Get some sleep! The thought of it infuriated him. Here he was, more than a thousand miles from home, no, more than a thousand years from home, about to face God knows what kind of danger, and he's told to try and get some sleep!

Why is it that adults always think they know more than kids? he stewed. *Wouldn't they be surprised if they knew the truth about me?* He considered this for a moment, wondering how they would react. *Would they help me? Or would they be afraid of me?* He knew that throughout much of history, people who were considered to be too different were often shunned or worse, beheaded or burned alive. He wondered how people in the twenty-first century would react if they found out about him and his strange ability to time travel. *They'd probably subject me to all kinds of tests,* he thought, *and they'd want to interview me on TV. My face would be splattered across the tabloids. I'd be famous. Photographers would follow me around and hide in bushes just to take my photo…* He shuddered as the reality came crashing in on him. *They'd eat me alive.* He drew his knees in to his chest and hugged them tightly. *People fear what they don't understand.* He decided that under no circumstances would he reveal his secret. Covering his eyes with his hands, he wished to be back at his grandparent's house. Even before he opened them he knew that nothing had changed. He stared intently at the door behind which George and Constantine had disappeared, wondering what secrets they shared. *I bet they're talking about the destruction of the cathedral and the fate of the Christian people. I just wish I could know for sure.* Hoping that it would provide him with some answers, he pulled the cross from over his head, held it in the palm of his hands, and stared intently at the inscription on the back.

Spera in Domino et fac bonum.

He frowned, contemplating the words. *Trust in the Lord and do good. If this is supposed to be a hint, it's not much help.* He ran his fingers through his hair in frustration. *Why am I here,* he kept wondering, *and how will I ever find my way home?* One thing was certain, he wasn't going to learn anything just sitting and doing nothing.

Hastily, he slid his cross back on and glanced toward the kitchen. Perpetua and Juliana were still busy. Rising quietly, he tiptoed toward the door and put his ear to it.

George was speaking in a raised voice. "…and while our emperor sits comfortably in his palace, surrounded by wealth and excess, many of his people starve!" he said angrily. "Desperation and poverty spread throughout the Empire like a plague, yet he remains blind to it because he worships the gods of greed and power, not love. Surely you realize that the Empire is sinking like a leaky ship at sea. Just as water bursts through a ship's gaping seams, so the barbarians invade our borders. Battle after battle is fought...to what end?"

"To what end?!" exclaimed Constantine. "We fight to preserve the mightiest empire on earth! Rome! Or do you no longer believe that Rome is worth fighting for?"

"I love Rome," retorted George, "but if I am forced to choose between Rome and God, I will choose God!"

"Even if it means certain death?!" asked Constantine incredulously.

"Choosing God will never mean death," argued George, "on the contrary, choosing God means life."

"That makes no sense!" said Constantine in exasperation. "Explain yourself!"

"Only God yields the power over life and death" explained George. "Our emperor can kill the flesh but not the spirit, and those who remain faithful to our Lord God will be rewarded with life everlasting in the Kingdom of Heaven."

"Is this true?" asked Constantine incredulously.

"Yes, Constantine. 'Tis true."

There was a moment of silence before Constantine continued. "George, be reasonable. Surely you must understand that our emperor is only trying to restore unity and peace to the Empire."

"Unity? Oh, Constantine, you're already beginning to sound like a caesar, or a bishop. It's absurd! Unity cannot be forced! And anyway, what about freedom? Must unity come at the price of freedom? Should we not have the right to worship as we please? Our emperor may believe that what he is doing is for the best, but truly I tell you, only an unworthy leader would force a man to turn his back on God." He paused before continuing in a lower voice. "Have you any idea how many men I've seen slaughtered on the battlefield? And as they lay suffering, awaiting death, who do you think was there to comfort them? Our emperor? His gods? No, Constantine. It was our loving and merciful Lord, Jesus Christ. The promise of his love is what gives men the strength to go on. In the end, our faith is all we have. Without it, we have nothing."

There was silence for a moment before Constantine asked, "How can you be so sure? What if you're wrong?"

"How can love be wrong?" said George.

Silence.

Daniel pressed his ear more firmly to the door. It sounded like someone was moving around. He tensed his body, preparing to run away quickly if the door began to open.

Finally Constantine spoke again. "If you refuse to offer him a sacrifice, he'll have you killed. He'll want to make an example of you."

"So be it," said George.

"So that's it then?" said Constantine incredulously. "You've made your decision? Is there nothing that I can say to make you change your mind and come with me?" he begged.

There was a moment of silence in which, Daniel was certain, George shook his head in a defiant "no" followed by, "But I want you to promise me something. Promise me that if you become emperor, you'll allow Christians the freedom to worship as they please."

"Without your help it's unlikely that I'll ever be emperor," shot Constantine. "I can't do it alone. Galerius Caesar will do whatever it takes to capture the throne. I was hoping to have you by my side to help lead the troops. Without you, who can I trust?"

"Keep your promise to me and you'll have the help of the all-powerful and ever-living God," said George. "With Him by your side, anything is possible." There was a long pause before George repeated, "Promise me, Constantine."

"As you wish, George. I swear it."

Daniel almost jumped out of his skin when a voice behind him whispered, "What are you doing?"

It was Perpetua; she was alone. When she saw the expression on his face she put her hand to her mouth to suppress a giggle.

"Would you quit sneaking up on me like that!" whispered Daniel indignantly.

"I'm sorry," she said. "I just came to find out if you want to come with me."

Daniel frowned. "Come with you where?"

"To the toilets," she said, and before he could ask his next question, she added, "Juliana's busy."

Daniel shifted his feet uneasily. "I don't think we're supposed to go anywhere. Can't you just use a chamber pot?" he suggested.

"I don't want to. I want to get some fresh air. Come on, Daniel, please," she begged.

He was torn between his desire to go and explore his new surroundings and his fear of disappointing George. While he hesitated Perpetua grew impatient.

"Oh forget it," she said, turning to leave. "I'll go without you."

He couldn't let her go alone. "Wait!" he called after her. "I'm coming!"

(XI)

Daniel shivered as he stepped out onto the cold, damp street. Holding his tiny clay lamp high, he peered warily into the darkness. A fog had rolled in, obscuring the moon overhead. The stillness of the night intensified the oppressive smells of raw sewage and burning wood. Up ahead, the road appeared deserted, but he could hear a crowd of people partying somewhere in the distance.

As they set out, he remained alert, his gaze shifting from side to side. He was thankful that there wasn't a breeze; he dreaded the idea of having to find his way home in the dark with no flame to light his way.

Beside him Perpetua strode along sure-footedly. "There should be a public toilet just around the corner here," she said.

Suddenly, the door to one of the shops flew open, and two disheveled men stumbled into their path reeking of too much wine. Instinctively, Perpetua and Daniel lowered their heads and set about circling around the men. Daniel was reminded of his Scout leader's sage advice: "When confronted with a wild animal, avoid eye contact and never turn your back." Unfortunately, these predators were not to be easily put off.

"Hey beautiful" one of them cajoled, "come 'ere."

With Daniel close at her side, Perpetua kept her head down and picked up her pace.

"Hey, I'm talking to you!" he shouted, indignant at being ignored. In a few strides he caught up with them, grabbed Perpetua roughly by the arm, and swung her around to face him.

"What's your problem?" he slurred. "Are you deaf?"

"Leave me alone," she pleaded, struggling to free her arm from his painful grip.

"Not a chance," he sneered and drew her in closer.

"Let go of her!" shouted Daniel. He pushed the man in the chest and grabbed Perpetua by the hand in an effort to help her break free. Suddenly, out of the darkness, the man's companion flew at Daniel, shoving him backwards into the dirt.

"Holy Mary, Mother of God, pray for us," breathed Perpetua.

Her assailant frowned. "What's she talking about?" he grumbled to his partner who staggered to his side.

"She's a Christian," the man grinned maliciously, revealing several rotten teeth. "They think they're better than the rest of us. Refuse to go to the games, them."

This was too much for Perpetua. She spat in his face and kicked her assailant hard in the groin. Quickly, before the men had time to react, Daniel grabbed her hand and ran at top speed, dragging her along with him. After a few blocks, when they were sure they weren't being followed, they stopped to catch their breath.

"I hope they all burn in hell," hissed Perpetua in between gasps.

Daniel took several deep, calming breaths. "What did he mean when he said that Christians refuse to go to the games?" he asked curiously.

"The gladiator games," answered Perpetua, matter-of-factly. "Why? Christians in Canada don't go to them, do they?"

"No, definitely not!" chuckled Daniel. "We're into hockey."

"What?"

"Oh, forget it."

The walk home was long and dark. Their lamp had gone out in the scuffle.

When they finally made their way back to the security of the apartment, George was waiting for them. He was visibly relieved by the sight of them. After lecturing the two of them on the dangers of going out after dark (like they needed it), he and Pasicrates left for the vigil.

Shortly afterwards, Daniel kneeled with Perpetua before the picture of the Good Shepherd and earnestly prayed for George's safe return.

(XII)

By the time he crawled into bed that evening, Daniel was so tired that he could barely keep his eyes open, and almost instantly, he fell asleep.

For several hours he slept peacefully, barely moving, his mind free of thoughts, his chest gently rising and falling with each new breath, but as the last burning candle spluttered and died, his eyelids began to twitch…

He was trapped in a dangerous land and was being chased by an evil dragon that sought to destroy his cross. Desperately, he ran…on and on…as fast as his legs would carry him, all the while clinging tightly to his cross for he knew that if the dragon succeeded in destroying it, he'd be captive forever. But still the dragon gained on him.

Suddenly, just as the great winged beast was about to swoop down upon him, George appeared at his side, on horseback, with his sword drawn. He swung at the dragon, grazing it with his blade.

"Run!" he yelled.

Daniel sprinted forward. The evil beast let out a blood-curdling shriek and opened its jaws wide in an attempt to devour George whole.

Just as Daniel thought that all hope was lost, the sky opened up and a brilliant white light descended upon him, banishing the darkness.

"Daniel, wake up!"

He opened his eyes to discover Pasicrates standing over him, a clay lamp in his hand. He sat up quickly, groping for the cross at his neck to make sure that it was still there, and rubbed the sleep from his eyes.

"Are you alright?" frowned Pasicrates.

At first, Daniel didn't answer; his mind was in a haze. Then slowly the events of the previous day came back to him, and he was overcome with a feeling of dread. "I'm fine," he lied.

Pasicrates stared at him curiously for a moment before turning to go. "'Tis the Lord's Day," he said. "We mustn't be late for Mass."

Daniel climbed out of bed and slid into his shoes. The cool morning air made him shiver slightly. He'd slept in his clothes and used his cloak for a pillow. He reached for it now and pulled it on, over his head. Before leaving the room, he quickly straightened the wool blanket on his bed. It was still dark out, but a flickering light shone in through the open door.

He found Perpetua in the kitchen leaning over a basin, splashing cold water on her face. Juliana was moving about the room, preparing for the day. She smiled when she saw him.

"How did you sleep?" she asked.

"Alright," he yawned.

Pasicrates sat in a chair by the wood-burning brazier, with his legs outstretched and his eyes closed. He looked exhausted.

"Where's George?" Daniel wondered aloud.

"At the vigil," said Juliana. "If you're thirsty, help yourself to some water. We shall be joining him shortly."

+

The moon shone overhead as they hurried along the deserted streets. To the east, the sky was beginning to lighten.

"It sure is quiet," commented Daniel. "What time is it?"

"Almost dawn," said Pasicrates, "but work is forbidden on the Festival of Terminalia. Soon after daybreak the city will come alive and the celebrations will begin."

As they drew nearer to the church they began to see other people walking quietly in the same direction.

"Do you think many people will come today?" Daniel asked.

Pasicrates shook his head solemnly. "Most will choose to worship the Lord in the secrecy of their homes." He paused briefly, before asking, "Tell me, Daniel, do you expect to see your parents at Mass?"

Daniel's face turned bright red. He stared down at the muddy ground beneath his feet, certain that Pasicrates suspected something. After hesitating for a few seconds, he mumbled, "No," and braced himself for an onslaught of questions and accusations. However, much to his relief, Pasicrates said nothing.

A couple of blocks later, the church came into sight. It looked nothing like any church that Daniel had ever seen. At first, he was surprised by its appearance, but then he remembered what the bishop had said about it being an old Roman temple that had fallen into disuse before being converted into a Christian church. It was old, white, and rectangular in shape, like a box, with a wide staircase at the front that ran the entire width of the building and tall pillars on either side of the entrance.

As they climbed the stairs and approached the front door, Daniel slowed down to let Perpetua go ahead of him.

Unsure of what to expect, he decided that the best course of action would be to follow her lead.

When he stepped inside, he felt as though he was passing into a different world. The change was abrupt, like diving into a pool of water. The air was warm and the enchanting sound of a beautiful hymn filled his ears. All the fear and anxiety he'd carried with him was washed away and replaced with peace and tranquility. He closed the door behind him and paused to examine his surroundings. Dozens of glowing candles flickered, casting shadows on the walls. A stone bench ran along the edge of the entire room, except at the front, where a tall rectangular table stood alone, covered in white linen. In front of this, several wooden chairs had been placed in a row. These were reserved for the bishop, priest, and deacons.*

Tucked away in a nook near the front of the room, a petite young woman stood alone, singing sweetly, with a candle in her hands. Daniel marveled that one voice could evoke so much emotion.

Quietly, people filed in and seated themselves. Several kneeled and bowed their heads in prayer.

Daniel took off his cloak and followed Perpetua and the others to a spot near the front, where George sat alone, silently praying. He was hunched forward with his elbows rested on his knees and his hands folded at his forehead. Their arrival jolted him back to reality. He smiled in greeting and moved over to make room for them.

Daniel relaxed and scanned the room, observing the crowd. The congregation was a diverse mix of people, men

---

* Because of it's association with paganism, incense was not burned on Christian alters until the latter part of the fourth century.

and women — mostly women — young and old. The majority of them looked like ordinary, hard working people, their skin lined and weather beaten, their clothes well worn, but a few in the crowd bore the unmistakable signs of wealth — jewelry, luxurious garments, and an entourage of neatly dressed servants.

A few times, he caught people staring in their direction and whispering behind their hands. George was a well-respected member of their community, and his return had not gone unnoticed.

Daniel jumped when all of a sudden loud, booming bells began ringing in the distance; the same bells that he'd heard the night before. He gave Perpetua a questioning look and leaned toward her.

"Yes," she whispered in his ear, "'tis the morning bells. The day has begun."

This had been the signal they'd all been waiting for. Simultaneously, the congregation stood and joined in singing a welcoming hymn while the bishop, priest, and deacons entered and took their places at the altar.

When the song ended, Bishop Anthimus held out his arms, palms facing upward, and began to chant.

"The grace of our Lord Jesus Christ, and the love of God the Father, and the communion of the Holy Spirit be with you all."

The congregation responded, chanting in unison. "Let us lift up our hearts."

Each time the congregation chanted Daniel did his best to mouth the words in silence. He was amazed by the familiarity of it all. He'd expected the Mass to have changed more over the course of seventeen hundred years.

"It is meet and right to worship Father, Son, and Holy Spirit," continued the bishop, "the Trinity one in essence and —"

Suddenly, the door at the back of the room burst open, and a young boy, about ten years of age with dark skin and curly hair, tumbled forward. He wore an old, patched cloak, and his expression was one of mingled fear and excitement. Wide-eyed and struggling to catch his breath, he scanned the room once before taking several timid steps forward toward the altar, where he stopped and bowed.

A whisper rippled through the crowd.

Bishop Anthimus hurried toward the boy. "Have you come bearing news, my son?" he asked.

"Yes, Bishop!" the young boy answered breathlessly. "The soldiers have just posted an edict! Sister Anna sent me to warn you!"

Agitated discussion broke out as the crowd struggled to grasp the meaning of his words. Perpetua reached for Daniel's hand and squeezed it tightly, with fear in her eyes.

"I don't understand," whispered Daniel. "What's an edict?"

"It's a proclamation!" she said, and seeing the look of confusion on his face added, "It's how the emperor announces new laws. He creates them at his whim."

Bishop Anthimus raised his hand calling for silence and the discussion trickled to a stop. The messenger boy stood nervously before him, fidgeting with the hem of his cloak and awaiting further instruction.

"Tell me, my son," implored Bishop Anthimus, laying his hands on the boy's shoulders and looking directly into his eyes, "do you know anything more about the edict?"

The room was completely silent now, all eyes glued to the young boy's face. He swallowed nervously and shook his head. "No. Only what I've told you."

George stepped forward, his fists clenched at his sides and his jaw set.

Bishop Anthimus looked over at him and frowned. When he spoke it was barely more than a whisper. "What is it, George?"

"The edict forbids Christianity."

A scene of panic and chaos followed. While a few in the crowd grabbed their cloaks and hurriedly prepared to leave, others raised their fists in protest.

From somewhere near the back of the room, a high, clear voice rang out. "He can't stop me from worshipping Christ! I would rather die!"

Daniel turned to see a stout, middle-aged woman with a defiant expression on her face. Her clothes were faded, and a young child rested comfortably on her swollen hip. Several more children were gathered around her skirt. Nearby, other members of the congregation were nodding fiercely and echoing their agreement. Across from Daniel, a frail old woman hung her face in her hands and wept.

In the midst of the chaos Bishop Anthimus and George remained frozen, staring at one another in silence. For one brief moment, the bishop clung desperately to the hope that it was all just some kind of a terrible misunderstanding. But a look can say a thousand words, and as he gazed into George's somber eyes, the harsh reality of what was to come came crashing in on him. And he was overcome with a feeling of dread.

The sound of footsteps heading toward the exit brought him back to his senses. "Wait!" he called. "Before you go, I beg you to listen."

Obediently, the congregation stopped and turned to face him, and the room once again fell silent.

His eyes blazed, but his voice was calm as he spoke. "Today, a shadow of darkness has been cast upon the Roman Empire by tyrants who seek to oppress the righteous. Do not lose faith, my children," he pleaded. "No matter what happens, remember God's promise...He is with us, even now."

He paused for a moment, his mind frantically searching for words that would adequately convey to them the power of God's love, words that would nourish and sustain them throughout the oncoming drought.

"There are two ways," he said, "the way of life and the way of death, but a great difference between the two. Ours is the way of life. No matter what horrors befall you, no matter what promises or threats that our emperor may make, you must never lose sight of this. When you find yourself alone and surrounded by darkness, you must cling to this knowledge and let it burn within your hearts, like a flame. Difficult times lie ahead. Death surrounds us; hatred, greed, envy, lust, selfishness, and fear all wait for you outside this door," he pointed dramatically toward the exit. Several people glanced over their shoulders nervously. The bishop paused. He wondered how many of them would suffer and die at the hands of the soldiers, and worse, how many would lose faith.

"In the days to come, your faith will be tested," he continued. "You will be urged to worship false idols, but you must not, for it is the service of dead gods! Instead, continue to love the God who made you," he implored, "and love your neighbour as yourself. Turn your back on vengeance and hatred, and bless those who curse you, and pray for your enemies, and fast for those who persecute you. For what reward is there for loving those who love you? Do not the Gentiles do the same? But love those who hate you, and you shall not have an enemy. No matter what challenges you may face," he said earnestly, "remain steadfast and accept whatever happens to you as good, knowing that apart from God nothing comes to pass."*

After blessing them one last time and leading them in a closing prayer, he bid them farewell. Most people gathered their belongings and straightaway fled for the safety of their homes, but some lingered to discuss the edict. Daniel and his companions were among them.

"It's as we'd feared, is it not?" Lactantius was saying in a hushed voice, his eyes darting to the door every now and then, as if he expected the soldiers to barge in on them at any moment. "We must convince Bishop Anthimus to gather the Holy Scriptures and flee, quickly, before it's too late."

"Did I hear my name?" said a voice behind them.

They looked up to see the bishop standing there.

"Yes," said George, "we were revisiting our conversation of last night. Have you made a decision? Will you go?"

"I prayed that it wouldn't come to this," said the bishop, folding his hands together and pressing them to his forehead.

---

* *The Didache,* trans. Roberts-Donaldson, http://www.early Christian writings.com /text/didache-roberts.html (accessed Feb. 12, 2007)

While George, Lactantius, and Pasicrates anxiously awaited his decision, other members of the congregation began to join them. Daniel and Perpetua hung back, trying not to be noticed. They didn't want to risk being sent home. The church was now almost empty. Father Paul and Deacon Adrian hurried about the altar, packing away what was left of the sacred items. Most had been destroyed along with the cathedral, and they hoped to save all those that remained.

Finally, the bishop opened his eyes. "Yes," he said, "I will go. But not before I've seen the edict."

"No, Bishop," groaned Lactantius. "You must go immediately! I can assure you that even as we speak the soldiers seek you!"

Bishop Anthimus raised his hand resolutely. "That may be so, my son, but I refuse to leave until I know exactly what it is that I am fleeing from."

Before Lactantius could argue any further, George interrupted him. "Then we have no time to waste. How long will it take for you to pack?" he asked the bishop.

"Not long. I leave my flock in the capable hands of Father Paul and Deacon Adrian. I need only pack some personal belongings and gather together whatever Scriptures I can take."

"Good. I too am curious to see this edict."

The crowd murmured in agreement.

"We must hurry!" repeated Lactantius urgently.

George nodded and turned toward the exit. As people began to file out he pulled the bishop aside and said privately, "No matter what happens, you must give me your word that after you've seen the edict you will make haste and escape Nicomedia as quickly as possible."

Bishop Anthimus studied him carefully. "Do not do anything rash, my son," he whispered. "Life is sacred."

George smiled grimly. "I can assure you, Bishop, that I've no death wish, but I've spent my entire life fighting to preserve my freedom. I don't intend to stop now." The two friends embraced one another, painfully aware that this farewell might be their last.

Lactantius was already at the door, peering out. "Come on," he urged.

When they emerged into the cool morning air, George finally became conscious of Perpetua and Daniel tagging along behind. "Where's Juliana?" he asked sternly.

"She left awhile ago," answered Perpetua. "She wanted to make sure that the young messenger boy made it home safely. She said she'd meet us back at the apartment."

While Daniel and Perpetua stood quietly before him, silently praying that they'd be allowed to go, George struggled over the decision. He'd hoped that Juliana could escort them home safely, but with that option gone, he was at a loss. While the crowd looked on impatiently, he turned to Pasicrates.

"What do you think?" he asked. "Should I send them home alone?"

Before Pasicrates could answer, Daniel shot him a pleading look. He wanted desperately to go with them and to see the edict for himself. He felt he must.

Pasicrates met his gaze momentarily before replying. "Why not let them come? They're old enough for the truth."

(XIII)

A thick layer of cloud had blown in, blotting out the early morning sun. Shivering, the small group of Christians hurried along a dreary maze of deserted streets toward the heart of the city.

George led the way. Unlike the others, who spoke incessantly about the edict, he remained silent, absorbed in his own thoughts.

Even after everything that had happened he still found it hard to believe that Emperor Diocletian would actually put an empire wide ban on Christianity. Throughout the first three centuries many Christians had suffered for their faith, but with the exceptions of Decius and Valerian, no emperor had ever tried to entirely wipe out the religion. In fact, many of the early persecutions hadn't involved the reigning emperor at all, but were instead the horrible result of an intolerant mob and local magistrate.

George recalled with unease the various manners in which the martyrs had been killed. Stoning, crucifixion, beheading, by fire…. He remembered the nightmares that he'd suffered as a young boy when he'd learned about Emperor Nero, who, in 64 A.D., had accused Christians of starting a massive fire that had ravaged through Rome destroying large sections of the city. Although there had been no evidence to support his claim, he'd ordered those arrested to be tied to posts and burned alive.

But that had been Nero, thought George bitterly, *an incompetent leader infamous for his selfishness and vanity. Surely Diocletian wouldn't be so cruel to his own people?!*

George had always admired Emperor Diocletian—his skill in the military field as well as his commitment to improving the lives of the Roman people. It was hard for him to accept the fact that his boyhood hero had become a ruthless tyrant.

Staring blankly at the road ahead, he ran his fingers through his hair in frustration. *How can a man with so much talent be so blinded to the truth?* he wondered. But he knew the answer, had known it for some time really. It was power—absolute power. Like so many leaders before him, Diocletian had become drunk on it and now could no longer see things as they really were.

George remembered with disgust, the lavish ceremony at which Diocletian had proclaimed himself to be the son of Jupiter, no longer a mortal man but instead a god, to be worshipped and adored as such. He realized now that this had been a defining moment in his reign, the beginning of the decline in the relations between he and his Christian subjects. After all, to them there was only one God, and He alone was worthy of their worship. But still, George had never expected things to go this far. He wondered now, how many Christians would be killed as a result of the edict? Hundreds, perhaps thousands? Only time would tell.

George's thoughts drifted back in time, to the day when he'd resigned from his post as a Tribune of the Imperial Guard...

Several months earlier...

George was alone in his room, packing up his belongings and preparing to leave Nicomedia, when a messenger arrived telling him that the emperor wished to see him. In recent years, Diocletian had made fewer and fewer public appearances, preferring instead to stay within the confines of his private chambers and to delegate his duties to one of his many assistants, so it was with a mixture of curiosity and dread that George set out on that warm summer evening.

When he reached the palace, he was met by a young, male servant who led him down a wide hall and into a vast, dimly lit room where several haughty looking clerks and dozens of slaves in identical crisp, white tunics waited impatiently for his arrival.

At the sight of him, a hush fell over the room and everyone hurried into position; clerks posing with pen and paper in hand, slaves lining the walls, or else stationing themselves several feet behind their masters, arms laden with scrolls and wax tablets, ready to answer their beck and call.

An obese eunuch* in a long, tent-like, silk tunic shuffled to George's side, ceremoniously announcing his arrival and commanding that he fall prostrate before his Lord and Master, Gaius Valerius Aurelius Diocletianus.

George was a practical man; he hated all the changes that had taken place at court, the increased pomp and ceremony. He longed for the old Diocletian, the one that used to stand and speak to his men eye to eye. Even so, he

---

* Eunuchs are men who were castrated before puberty, rendering them asexual. They were highly valued as slaves and servants and were often found in the imperial court.

lowered himself dutifully onto the polished mosaic tiles and lay face down as Diocletian entered the room, surrounded by his imperial guard, and seated himself proudly on his golden throne.

The silence that followed was almost unbearable. George hated the unnerving sensation of Diocletian's eyes on the back of his neck.

Finally, Diocletian spoke. "Stand up, George," he commanded, "and come forward."

As George rose to his feet, he stole a quick glance into the emperor's face and was alarmed to find that he looked paler and thinner than usual, but he reminded himself that it was late in the day and that things always look different by candlelight.

He listened patiently as Diocletian tried to persuade him to stay on in his post as a tribune, but when he was finally given the opportunity to speak, he told the emperor that his decision remained unchanged and that he would not make the required sacrifice to the Roman gods.

Diocletian became furious. He accused him of disrespect and went on for what seemed like hours about the lack of discipline among the Christian soldiers and about what he described as "their dangerous disregard of the gods."

George tried to explain to him about the One True God and the Ten Commandments, but it was useless. Like his rule, Diocletian's mind was unbending. However, to George's great relief, he confessed that he was hesitant to push the Christians too far.

"The spread of Christianity must be stopped," he said, "for it threatens to destroy the Empire. I'm not an animal, George. I do not wish to see blood shed needlessly. All I ask is that Christians show the proper respect for the gods, and offer the necessary sacrifices. Is that so much?"

George kept his eyes focused on the floor and waited for him to continue.

"For the good of the Empire, George, I implore you to show an outward display of loyalty to the gods by making a public sacrifice. By the sun our god, and the victory of all the gods, if you listen to me, George, if you obey my will, I will give you much property and make you second in my kingdom."*

The words stung.

Forgetting protocol, George raised his eyes from the floor and looked up for a moment into those of the emperor, and in that moment he felt as though a veil had suddenly been lifted and that he was seeing him clearly for the very first time. It was a sad moment for George because he realized just how far Diocletian was from understanding. It was like watching a man drifting helplessly out to sea and knowing that he is beyond reach. Defeated, he lowered his gaze and shook his head.

"It would be blasphemy," he said.

Diocletian leaned forward and slammed his fist on the arm of his throne. "Why must you be so unrelenting!" he shouted.

George said nothing.

Diocletian glared down at him in silence for a moment and took several deep breaths in an effort to gain control of his raging nerves. When he finally spoke again, it was in a voice of forced calm.

"I've heard about your martyrs and their willingness to suffer and die in the name of Jesus the Nazarene. It worries

---

* George Anton Kiraz, ed., *Acts of Saint George,* trans, E.W. Brooks (New Jersey: Gorgias Press, 2006) 43.

me. If I try and force them, I risk killing thousands and thus creating an even greater divide within the Empire."

A sudden gust of wind whipped at George's cloak, sending a chill through his body and snapping him out of his reverie. *I can't believe that was only last summer*, he thought, rubbing his hands together to warm them. *It's amazing how quickly things can change. Diocletian was in no mood to kill Christians back then. Still, I should have recognized the warning signs. I should never have left the city.*

When George had departed for Palestine, he'd remained hopeful that Diocletian would let go of the idea of forcing all Romans to worship the state gods. But when news had reached him that Galerius Caesar had wintered by the emperor's side, he'd known that things would go from bad to worse. After all, it was a well-known fact that Galerius despised Christians; next to him, Nero looked like a pussycat.

At the thought of him, George narrowed his eyes and clenched his fists unconsciously. He couldn't help wondering how things would have turned out if only Galerius had been occupied in other parts of the Empire. *Oh well*, he sighed, *there's no point in worrying about what might have been. What matters now is that it's been done. The edict has been posted. The emperor has taken his stand, and now I must take mine.*

His thoughts were interrupted when a drop of rain splattered on his cheek. And then another. Turning his attention toward the sky, he saw dark threatening clouds gathering in the distance. A storm was brewing.

He was startled when a young voice next to him groaned.

"Oh, great…now it's starting to rain." It was Daniel.

George looked over at him and smiled. He was intrigued by the boy and by his strange situation. He wondered what he'd been doing all alone, so far from home. Surely he'd been accompanied by his father, or by trusted servants. Long distance journeys were far too dangerous for boys his age to do alone. But then, what had become of them? He was frustrated by the fact that Daniel was unable to provide him with any answers.

He surveyed him shrewdly now. It was possible that he'd suffered a head injury, perhaps from being thrown from a horse. That would explain his confusion and memory loss. But he doubted it. Although he liked the boy, he couldn't help but feel that there were things he wasn't telling them. And it wasn't just the way in which they'd found him that was puzzling; there was something else odd about him. He asked the strangest questions. It gave one the impression that he was a complete stranger to the Empire. But that was impossible. As far as George knew there were no Christians beyond the western borders, only barbarism and brutality. And then there was that cross that he wore...

"Daniel," he said, "are you still wearing your cross?"

Daniel looked up at him and nodded.

"Let me see it."

If it was anyone else, Daniel would have said "no," but he trusted George. Without hesitating, he pulled it out from under his tunic and handed it over. He wondered what had caused George's sudden interest in his cross and whether he might know something about its mysterious powers. *Maybe he can help me!* he thought hopefully.

While George studied the cross, Daniel walked alongside him, struggling to keep up with his long strides. When he came across the Latin inscription on the back, George stopped dead in his tracks.

"What is it?" asked Daniel.

"'Tis Scripture," murmured George, turning the cross over in his hand and staring at it.

Although crosses had been around for centuries and were used as symbols by many ancient cultures, in the early fourth century they weren't commonly associated with Christianity. George was deeply moved by the craftsmanship and beauty of Daniel's silver cross and the inscription proved, beyond a doubt, that whoever created it had intended it to be a reminder of God's endless love.

While Daniel stood impatiently watching, George stared transfixed at the cross still clutched in his palm. Finally, he tore his eyes away and looked into Daniel's watchful face.

"How did you come by this?" he asked.

"My grandfather gave it to me," said Daniel. "He said that—" he faltered, unsure of how to continue. He was going to say that it had belonged to St. George, but then he remembered who he was talking to.

George looked at him curiously, his eyebrows raised. "Go on," he prodded.

"He said that it had belonged to a brave saint," finished Daniel.

"Did he?" said George. He wondered if it were true. Perhaps it was. It was certainly very valuable, an odd thing for a boy to be wearing while traveling the Roman countryside.

"Do you know anything about it?" asked Daniel hopefully. "Does it look familiar to you?"

Before George could reply, someone up ahead called out his name. He looked up to discover that he and Daniel had fallen behind. Several of the men were urging him forward. After giving them a quick wave to let them know he'd be along, George turned back to Daniel. "I'm afraid I must go."

He slung the cross gently over Daniel's neck, letting it come to rest against his outer garment. "Listen," he paused, struggling to find the right words, wondering what on earth he could say to prepare the boy for the coming horrors. There was no telling how bad things would soon get, or how many innocent people would suffer. He reached out and touched the cross. "Remember and draw strength from the saints," he said, "including the one that once wore this cross."

As he walked away, Daniel fought the impulse to reach out and grab a hold of the back of his cloak and warn him. *Of what though?* he thought, helplessly. *What can I possibly say? Watch out for the dragon? Have your lance ready?*

Around the next corner the road opened up, and he found himself once again gazing in awe at the many tall buildings and monuments that lined the forum. It was much quieter than it had been the previous evening; the boisterous crowds had disappeared leaving a cold and lonely silence in their wake. The only other detectable signs of life were a scavenging dog and a flock of birds, which fluttered here and there pecking at discarded bits of food littering the ground.

Before long, distant voices were carried their way on the bitter wind and a massive white temple surrounded by bustling people rose into sight. Hundreds of servants dressed in drab grey tunics were busy preparing for the ancient rituals and celebrations that would be held throughout the day. Today was the Festival of Terminalia, and Emperor Diocletian was determined to make it a day to remember. While it was not uncommon for Roman emperors to provide free food, wine, and entertainment, on this particular holiday Diocletian had outdone himself. It was, after all, the day that he had chosen to put an end to the Christian cult, and he intended to remind his people of the majesty and authority of the Roman gods.

Spread out among the emperor's servants, lazily lounging and barking out the odd command, were what Daniel considered to be an alarming number of soldiers. *Why so many?* he wondered fearfully.

He was so absorbed in the activities unfolding around him that he almost fell over a couple of soldiers squatting next to a smoldering fire, their hands outstretched for warmth. The men glared at him as he clumsily regained himself and muttered an apology before continuing on his way. He chanced a quick glance back and was relieved to see they'd resumed their position as though undisturbed.

"I wouldn't do that again," warned Perpetua.

"I don't plan on it," said Daniel. "It's hard to avoid them though. They're everywhere."

"Tell me about it," agreed Perpetua. "My mother used to say that if we took the money from the wages of the soldiers and used it to feed the poor, no one would go hungry!"

Daniel smiled grimly. The reminder of Perpetua's dead mother did nothing to calm his uneasy stomach. In an attempt to change the subject he asked, "Where exactly are we going, anyway?"

"The Basilica," she responded, pointing directly ahead to a towering building, which was fronted by polished marble stairs and tall white pillars. "The offices of the emperor are inside. The edict will be posted to the front door."

As they drew nearer the knot inside Daniel's stomach grew larger. He noticed with unease that soldiers had begun to whisper amongst themselves and point in their direction, but still he marched on and before long found himself standing at the top of the stairs alongside many other Christians who were already gathered there.

(XIV)

They were not alone. Stationed on either side of the doors were several stony faced Imperial Guards dressed in crimson cloaks and plated armour, their swords gleaming at their sides. These were elite soldiers whose primary duty was to guard the emperor. They stood silently now, unmoving and watchful, as though waiting for a signal.

When Bishop Anthimus reached the top of the stairs the crowd parted to make way for him, and he hurried forward, anxious to read the edict. He was almost to the doors when one of the guards broke from the ranks and stepped menacingly in his path, forcing him to an abrupt halt. The two men stood nose to nose, the young guard gripping hungrily onto the hilt of his sheathed sword and glaring into the bishop's calm face, daring him to pass. A heavy tension fell over the crowd. For several long seconds no one moved, not even the guards, though beneath their armour, their bodies had grown taught, ready to pounce.

"I recognize you," sneered the soldier. "You're a Christian."

Bishop Anthimus opened his mouth to affirm his faith but was distracted by a flurry of movement in the nearby crowd. He turned just in time to see George emerge and plant himself at his right hand side. The young guard deflated at the sight of him. His face turned bright pink, and he took a step backwards, releasing his grip on the hilt of his sword and letting his hand fall to his side.

"Is there a problem, Lucius?" George asked calmly.

The young guard struggled to mask his hatred and contempt. Until recently George had been his superior, and years of legionary training cannot be undone overnight.

"No, Sir. No problem," he said, stepping back into line among the other soldiers, a couple of whom were trying, without much success, to suppress satisfied smirks.

Daniel edged his way away from the soldiers, into the centre of the crowd. It was then that he caught his first glimpse of the edict which was hand written on a scroll and nailed to the door. He craned his neck in an effort to read it but it was hopeless; there were too many people standing in his way. Bishop Anthimus and several other men, including George and Pasicrates, had gathered around it and were pouring over its contents. After several moments, the bishop stepped aside and stared blankly into the distance, his face dark and brooding.

"What does it say?" called out a man in the crowd. At first, Daniel was surprised by the question, after all, the man was close enough to read it himself, but then it dawned on him that many of these people were probably illiterate. George tore the edict from the door and turned to face the crowd.

"By order of Emperor Diocletian," he shouted, "it is hereby commanded that all churches be razed to the ground and that all Scriptures be destroyed by fire!" The crowd gasped. Those standing alongside Daniel drew the sign of the cross on their foreheads.

"Furthermore," continued George, "it has been commanded that all sacred vessels be confiscated and that, from this time forward, all meetings of Christian worship be forbidden!" Several in the crowd booed in protest. Daniel glanced over his shoulder in apprehension toward the guards who continued to stand by, watchful and silent. He immediately spotted the one called Lucius whispering treacherously into the ear of one of the other guards. Then, the guard to whom Lucius had spoken slipped quietly away and disappeared through the great wooden doors, into the Basilica. Daniel had an awful feeling that something terrible was about to happen but was distracted by George's booming voice as he continued to read.

"All Christians who hold places of rank and honour will lose their places and their privileges and all Christian freedmen will be re-enslaved!"

"He can't do that!" yelled a woman from somewhere behind Daniel. He turned and in so doing, noticed Bishop Anthimus and Lactantius making their way back down the stairs. The bishop appeared to be leaving rather reluctantly; Lactantius was urging him along by the elbow. Inside the bishop's head, a battle was raging. The part of him that knew that he must go, must escape this madness, was battling against that part of him that wished to stay and stand alongside George and defend the good name of Jesus Christ. But he walked on, with the knowledge that this was to be his role in the battle against tyranny; he was to protect the Holy Scriptures from destruction. He knew this because he had kneeled in prayer for hours, seeking direction from God, and the Great One had given him the guidance which he had sought. He was to take the scriptures and flee to the wilderness, where he would contact the Desert Fathers, those holy men and women who had fled the immorality and corruption of Roman society to seek refuge and solace in a life devoted entirely to prayer and a deeper understanding of God.*

Daniel watched them until they disappeared around a corner, and then he turned his attention back to George.

"Christians will no longer be permitted to press charges in cases of personal injury, adultery, or theft." he shouted bitterly, gripping the scroll tightly in his shaking fist.

"He's taken away our legal rights!" wailed the crowd.

"All Christian clergy will be put under arrest," he continued, "and only if they offer a sacrifice to the gods will they be set free from prison!"

The crowd gasped in shock.

"Furthermore," shouted George, raising his voice even louder in an effort to make himself heard over their wailing, "all Roman citizens will henceforth be required to give a public sacrifice to the gods on the pain of death!"** Daniel felt weak in the knees. While all around him people wept in shock and outrage, George's final words kept reverberating in his head...*on the pain of death!*

"These are the triumphs of Goths and Sarmatians!"*** roared the man next to him.

"But what does this mean?" cried a young woman tearfully. "Must we forsake God?"

"What choice do we have?" the man behind her responded bitterly. "I have a family to feed."

"He has no right to do this," breathed George, his face flushed in anger, the scroll still clenched firmly in his fist.

---

* This was the earliest form of Christian monasticism.

** In reality, the edicts weren't posted all at once, but in stages over several months.

*** Lactantius, *Of the Manner in which the Persecutors Died*, 13, http://www.new advent.org/fathers/ 0705.htm (accessed Mar. 24, 2007)

"He has every right," retorted the man grimly. "He's our emperor."

"There are laws greater than his," George reminded him, "those of our Lord and our God, and it's to those laws that we must abide." With a look of contempt, he held out the scroll and deliberately tore it in half, and then in half again. While the pieces tumbled to the ground, the crowd around him roared their approval.

At that moment the doors to the Basilica burst open and a long line of Imperial Guards began to file out, marching in pairs. Daniel recognized one of them as being the same guard who had disappeared several moments earlier. The unexpected arrival of such force had a silencing effect on the Christians. They backed out of the way to allow room for the growing number of soldiers who were now lining up in two rows, one on each side of the open doorway. George alone remained calm, rooted to his spot.

When the last soldier had emerged and taken his place in line next to the others, their commanding officer barked out an order calling them to attention. As they stood erect, all eyes straight ahead, a tall and imposing looking man wearing a long velvety cloak and heavy gold rings on his fingers swept through the doors and into their midst. His eyes were cold like ice, and he wore a neatly trimmed beard, which did nothing to hide his double chin. Daniel shrank back in fear. He knew who this man was, even before Perpetua put her lips to his ear and whispered almost inaudibly, "Galerius Caesar." A chill ran through Daniel's body as he watched him approach George with a look of pure hatred on his face.

"So it's true, you have returned," he sneered. George returned his icy stare and nodded his head slightly in acknowledgment.

"You'd have been better off to stay away," continued Galerius. "Things have changed in your absence." He smiled smugly and in a voice loud enough for everyone to hear, added, "I presume that you're here to read the emperor's new edicts?"

"I've read them," said George, motioning toward the ground underfoot where the torn edict lay scattered. "They change nothing."

Galerius looked down and gasped. "How dare you!" he roared. In one swift motion he raised his jeweled hand high and swung it powerfully against the side of George's head. George staggered slightly from the blow. Instinctively, Daniel tried to run forward to his defense but was stopped by Pasicrates, who gripped him firmly by the shoulder, refusing to let go. Blood trickled slowly down the side of George's face, and his chest heaved in fury. But he clenched his fists tightly and willed himself to remain calm, to resist the temptation to strike back. Several of the guards shifted their feet and glared mutinously at their caesar, but Galerius, in his rage, was oblivious to it.

"Don't just stand there you idiots!" he shouted at them. "Arrest him!" Two guards stepped forward and brusquely grabbed George by the arms.

"You may have found favour with the emperor," Galerius hissed into his face, "but I will have your head." Then, to the guards, he commanded, "Take him to the prison and leave him there until I consider how to destroy him and make havoc of his fair boyhood."*

---

* George Anton Kiraz, ed., *Acts of Saint George,* trans, E.W. Brooks (New Jersey: Gorgias Press, 2006) 36.

The women in the crowd burst into tears as George was led away, followed closely by Galerius Caesar and his entourage of soldiers.

As the guard at the back of the line was closing the great wooden doors, a young Christian man ran at him in a desperate attempt to break his way through, but the guard pushed him away and, after glancing quickly over his shoulder, begged of them, "Please, go home. There's nothing that you can do."

Then the doors were closed, and he was gone.

(XV)

Daniel was in shock. Later, looking back on it, he barely remembered the walk home, only that the rain poured down, soaking his hair and clothes. Normally he hated getting wet, but on that day he'd welcomed it. The coldness had helped to numb the pain that was swelling up inside him.

When they finally reached the apartment, Deacon Adrian and Juliana were already there, waiting for them. They hurried them inside, anxious to know what had become of George. The scene that followed was all a blur to Daniel. He had the strangest sensation that he was no longer standing in the entrance, shivering and dripping wet, but was instead hovering above looking down on the whole scene—Perpetua throwing herself into Juliana's arms and crying uncontrollably, and Pasicrates, looking old, pale, and bedraggled as he tried to explain the awful reality. Deacon Adrian insisting that they change into dry clothes before they catch the fever, and Juliana handing him some clothes (a slightly worn tunic and leggings that she'd picked up earlier that day from the orphanage) and leading him to a room to change. A small room, empty but for a stuffed mattress in the corner. The room he'd slept in. *Was that last night?* he wondered. It seemed like so long ago. He sat down on the bed and closed his eyes.

"Daniel…"

It was Pasicrates telling him to hurry up and to come and eat. He said that it would make him feel better. So he did, and it did. He sat next to Perpetua, ate warm bread and sipped on a hot, soothing, herbal drink that Juliana had prepared, and listened as the adults talked. He learned that Bishop Anthimus had been to the apartment shortly before they'd arrived and had managed to collect some of the Holy Scriptures. *Well, that was something…a drop of white surrounded by black.* There was nothing left to do but pray. Tomorrow would be a new day. Tomorrow they would meet with some of the other Christians, and they would decide how and where they would continue to worship their Messiah. But not today. Today they would pray.

So it was that on that fateful day, as the rest of the Empire ate, drank, and were merry, the Christians gathered in their homes and, on bended knees, earnestly prayed for justice.

(XVI)

In the days following George's arrest, Daniel went crazy trying to figure out a way to get back home. At first, he tried hiding in his bedroom at Juliana and Deacon Adrian's, squeezing his cross desperately between his two hands and begging to go home. *Please, God! Why are you doing this to me?!* he cried.

Eventually, after several wasteful hours in this state of self-pity, his fear gave way to anger, and in a rage he threw his cross against the wall. It landed on the floor in the corner of his room where it lay untouched and abandoned for three whole days. When Pasicrates noticed that it was missing and asked him where it was, he merely shrugged his shoulders and threw him what he hoped was his grouchiest frown.

However, by the third day, when he'd finally calmed down enough to see things clearly again, he realized how much he needed the cross and was overcome with a feeling of utter panic. He rushed to his room and, to his great relief, found it waiting for him exactly where he'd left it.

The following evening, in one final, last-ditch attempt to get back home, he tried reenacting the events of the night that had brought him there. It was a blustery, rainy night, and just before midnight he climbed out of bed, put on his clothes and pendant, and quietly snuck out of the apartment into the darkness outside. He stood alone on the muddy road, with the hood of his cloak pulled up tight over his head, and waited. Unfortunately, the only thing that happened was that his feet got soaked and he caught a nasty chill.

After that he stopped obsessing over trying to find a way home. He was still homesick, that never changed, but he no longer felt frustrated or angry or frightened. As he pulled off his wet cloak on that cold, blustery night and climbed back into bed, he realized something that he'd really known all along but had been unwilling to accept; for some mysterious reason, his fate was linked directly to George's. He still didn't know exactly what that meant. As he drifted off to sleep he wondered about what role he was to play. Was he a mere spectator or should he be doing something? And he wondered about George. How was he? What horrors would he face before this was all over? That was the night that Daniel finally stopped feeling sorry for himself and turned his attention outward.

+

George was still in prison but he wasn't alone. His defiance of the new edicts had inspired others to also stand up for what they believe in, and before long the prisons and limestone quarries were overflowing with Christians.[*]

Gangs of soldiers now patrolled the streets. When ordered, people were expected to scatter incense upon burning coals at the foot of a moving altar on which sat a divine image of their Lord and Master, Emperor Diocletian. Those who refused were arrested, and those who were most

---

[*] Many of those who were forced to work in the quarries were blinded by the persistent glare of the hot sun on the white limestone.

vocal in their opposition were subjected to public torture and execution. An uneasy tension settled over the city. No longer sure whom to trust, most Christians chose to retreat indoors and seek safety in the shelter of their homes. But even there they weren't safe; soldiers were known to barge in suddenly, day or night, and raid people's homes in search of holy books or sacred items. In the eastern half of the Empire, where Daniel was trapped, the persecutions were by far the bloodiest.

Almost daily, Pasicrates would return home just before sunset with new information concerning the peaceful rebellion of the Christian people and the related arrests. Diocletian's worst fears were coming true; despite the arrests and the tortures, many Christians continued to show no sign of giving in. Instead, the persecution appeared to be backfiring. The resistance of the Christian people and their unwavering faith in God's love was giving new hope to the poor and the suffering. Rather than die out, Christianity was driven underground, and from there it was spreading like a fire through a dead forest. In response, Diocletian doubled up on his efforts to wipe out The Way. Churches were destroyed, sacred books and artifacts were burned, and the clergy were hunted down and thrown into prison. While Galerius Caesar would have been happy to see every single Christian burned and their ashes thrown into the sea*, Emperor Diocletian continued to hold out hope that if the wealthy Christians could be swayed through intimidation, then others would follow. So he ordered his soldiers to seek out the rich, those who held places of high status and who

---

* This was considered blasphemous because of the Christian belief in the resurrection of the body.

owned land and property, and to try and force them to recant their faith. He threatened to take away their status and to confiscate their land, and if that didn't work, he resorted to torture, anything to get them to obey his will. Some did sway of course, but others did not. Those who were brave enough to stand by their convictions were condemned to death by fire or beheading or were fed to wild beasts in front of a cheering crowd. These were frightening times, and Daniel was a witness to it all. Knowing that he could not escape, he did what any boy would do, he learned to draw comfort from those around him and to try to settle into his new life as best he could.

(XVII)

Winter gave way to spring. The days grew longer, the sun warmed the air, and nature burst into renewed life. Despite the ongoing persecutions, Daniel managed to settle into a comfortable routine. Not long after George was arrested, Pasicrates had arranged for him and Perpetua to spend their days working at St. Mary's Orphanage, a large home in central Nicomedia that had been donated to the Church by a wealthy Christian family and that now housed nineteen orphans ranging in age from three months to twelve years. He and Perpetua had been working there for several weeks now and had come to think of it as a second home.

From the moment they'd walked in the door on their first day, Perpetua had fallen in love with the twins, a couple of mischievous three year old boys whose mother had died in childbirth and who Daniel had appropriately nicknamed "the terrible twosome." They weren't really terrible, even Daniel had to admit that most of the time they were pretty cute, but they were little fireballs of energy who enjoyed running around the house naked all day (they simply refused to stay clothed), leaving a path of destruction in their wake. Perpetua was the only person with the stamina to keep up with them, so it had been a natural decision to assign her the exhausting task of chasing after them, a job that she embraced.

As for Daniel, when he'd first learned that they'd be working at the orphanage, he'd had mixed feelings. He loved kids, but he'd also had horrible visions of snotty noses and dirty diapers. So when Anna, the grey haired widow who ran the household, had assigned him the task of helping the children with their studies, he'd been immensely relieved. Most of his time was spent helping a small group of seven-to-ten-year-olds with their reading and writing, but on several occasions he'd had the opportunity to listen to the older boys practice their public speaking, something which the roman's considered to be an essential part of a young man's education. He got along well with the kids and quickly felt at ease in his new environment. He'd been curious to find out what types of books the students would be reading and was surprised to find that it wasn't all Scripture, but was instead largely philosophy and poetry. Anna wasn't impressed when she discovered how little he knew of Plato's philosophy.

"What do they teach you in the west?" she'd scolded. "I suppose they think you're better off practicing your swordsmanship?" Daniel merely shrugged his shoulders mutely under her glare and prayed that she wouldn't ask him to demonstrate his swordsmanship in front of the class.

On a rainy afternoon, about ten days after he'd started there, Daniel discovered why so little time was spent studying Scripture when the door suddenly burst open and a gang of soldiers barged in and started rummaging through the house, tearing apart rooms and overturning furniture. That was his first experience with a raid. It had been hard for him to stand back and let the soldiers bully their way around the house. More than once he'd stepped forward, red in the face, prepared to tell one of them off, but was stopped by a warning look from Anna. From his perspective, this type of treatment was inherently wrong. It was an infringement on their rights. He had to remind himself that he was no longer in a democratic country, where citizens had earned the right to expect certain basic freedoms: the rule of law, the right to vote in fair elections, freedom of speech, freedom of the press, and freedom of religion. For the first time in his life he thought about all of the people who lived in parts of the world where no such freedom had yet been established.

When the soldiers left, Anna had taken him aside and warned him that under no circumstances was he to get in their way.

"Just let them conduct their searches," she'd said. "I don't want anyone getting hurt. Your lives mean more to me than the furnishings. And anyway" she'd leaned forward and whispered confidentially, "they'll never find anything of value."

On the days that followed, Daniel often wondered just where it was that she hid all of her sacred artifacts and writings, but he didn't bother to ask. He knew that she would never tell—ever.

+

At the end of each day, before the evening bell tolled, he and Perpetua would head home to Deacon Adrian and Juliana's where they would sit and, after giving thanks, eat their daily bread and sip hot apple tea in the warm glow of a single oil lantern, listening anxiously as Pasicrates, Juliana, and Deacon Adrian shared all of the latest news concerning the persecutions. What Daniel was most eager for was news concerning George. But none ever came.

"He's still in prison," Pasicrates would say patiently each evening. "Emperor Diocletian is hoping that he'll change his mind."

As the days turned to weeks Daniel began to grow impatient. He was tired of waiting and not knowing. He was beginning to feel as though he'd been sentenced to an eternity in purgatory.

Finally, one evening while he sat alone with Pasicrates and Deacon Adrian (Perpetua and Juliana had gone to the public bath), he decided to press for more information.

"But why?" he asked. "Why is he keeping George in prison for so long? He must realize by now that he'll never change his mind."

"He's scared," said Deacon Adrian through a mouthful of bread.

"What do you mean?" Daniel persisted.

"George is well loved," explained Pasicrates. "Diocletian doesn't want to kill him if he doesn't have to. It might cause a backlash."

Daniel frowned. "How much more of a backlash could there be? I still don't understand." Pasicrates set down his spoon and turned resignedly toward Daniel. He'd always known that this moment would come, the moment when he could no longer hide the awful truth from this mysterious boy who seemed to possess wisdom beyond his years. Up until then, he'd avoided the topic of George because he'd known where the conversation would lead, and he wasn't sure how Daniel would react when he found out. He considered him for a moment wondering how best to handle the situation. In the end he decided to give Daniel what he wanted — the truth.

"George is no ordinary man, Daniel. He's a soldier…an exceptionally skilled one. His bravery and leadership on the battlefield have earned him the loyalty and respect of all the soldiers who've ever fought alongside him. He holds a special place in the hearts of many, even our emperor. Diocletian now finds himself in a very difficult position. If George continues to defy the new edicts he can't set him free, that'll make him look weak, but if he kills him he risks angering his legions and having them turn against him. Either way, he's faced with a difficult decision. He can't risk losing the love and loyalty of his soldiers; his power depends on it. He may call himself a god, Daniel, but he knows as well as we do that his power really lies in the strength of his legions. If it didn't, there wouldn't be so many soldiers."

"Nor would they be paid so well," grumbled Deacon Adrian.

"True," agreed Pasicrates, "he must keep them happy. Unfortunately, history has proven that this is no easy task. Roman soldiers are fickle; their loyalties have been known to sway overnight from one side to the other. Diocletian hasn't killed George because he's afraid of what might happen if he does."

"But George doesn't want to be emperor," said Daniel. "He won't try and sway the soldiers."

"No, George doesn't want to be emperor, but there are others who do. Being the emperor of Rome is a dangerous job. There are constantly sharks circling, waiting for the right moment to strike."

"But then, how long will he keep George prisoner?" asked Daniel. "He can't keep him locked up forever. What's he waiting for?"

Suddenly, Deacon Adrian plunked his heavy wooden bowl down with a loud thud and shoved it aside disagreeably, causing fish stew to slop over the edges and spill onto the table. The unexpected noise made Daniel jump in his seat. He looked over in alarm at Deacon Adrian, whose face was now buried miserably in his hands.

"What is it?" he said, glancing fearfully from one man to the other. "What's the matter?" For a few minutes, no one spoke. Finally, Deacon Adrian withdrew his face from behind his hands.

"They're torturing him, boy!" he said miserably. "Don't you see?! They're doing every horrific thing imaginable to try and make him change his mind!"

Daniel felt as though he'd been punched hard in the stomach. He looked to Pasicrates for confirmation, hoping with all his heart that it wasn't true, but Pasicrates merely nodded his head sadly. A whole range of emotions washed over Daniel like a tidal wave—anger, sorrow, pity, fear. The effect was numbing. At first he couldn't speak; when he finally did, his tone was bitter.

"What exactly are they doing to him?" he asked. Neither man said a word. Deacon Adrian opened his mouth to speak but then changed his mind and instead spun around and stormed from the room. A few seconds later Daniel heard the front door slam shut. He stared at Pasicrates wide eyed.

"Tell me!" he demanded.

"I honestly don't know, Daniel. Not for sure anyway."

Daniel clenched his fists. He felt oddly hollow inside and his eyes were beginning to burn.

"Listen to me," said Pasicrates calmly. "I don't want you to worry about it. There's nothing that you, nor I, nor anyone else can do. This is a battle that George must fight alone. All we can do is pray that God will give him the strength to withstand all of the torments that are being thrown at him."

Daniel went to bed that night feeling sick with grief. For hours he lay in bed thinking about George. Finally, long after midnight, he drifted into an uneasy sleep. His head was filled with horrible visions of knights battling dragons, searing hot fire and swinging chains, bones breaking and flesh tearing, and faceless people screaming and begging for mercy.

When he awoke the next morning he was tired and his head throbbed, but he knew what he had to do.

(XVIII)

"If I tell you something, will you promise not to tell anyone?" whispered Daniel. He and Perpetua were alone in the central courtyard of the orphanage. It was late afternoon. He was supposed to be inside supervising some of the orphans while they studied, but he'd snuck out to try and have a private word with Perpetua while she spread clean laundry out to dry.

It was a warm, spring day. Nearby, a bee buzzed noisily in the herb garden. The sun shone brightly overhead in a clear, blue sky. The normally bustling household was quiet now, but soon the youngest children would awaken from their afternoon naps and the house would once again come to life. This had become Daniel's favourite time of the day, but it hadn't always been. Initially, he'd scoffed at the idea of taking a midday nap. After all, he came from a world in which napping was associated with laziness, a world which had become so busy that even Sundays were no longer set aside as a day of rest. "Rat race" was what his grandmother called it. How many times had he heard her telling his parents to stop working so much? "You've got to learn to take a break," she'd often say. "All you do is work, work, work…and for what?"

A door slammed shut somewhere in the distance causing Daniel to glance nervously over his shoulder.

"Of course," said Perpetua, holding up a tiny pair of wool leggings and squeezing out the excess water before laying them in the sun. "What is it?"

"I'm going to visit George," he whispered.

Perpetua stopped what she was doing and stared at him. "When?"

"Today, after work. I just wanted you to know in case something happens to me and...you know," he swallowed nervously, "and I don't make it home."

"Are you sure about this?" she whispered. "It sounds a little like walking straight into the lions' den."

"Yeah," he nodded. "I've thought it over and I'm sure. I need to see him." He reached for his cross and fiddled with it unconsciously before continuing in a lowered voice. "I need to see for myself that he's still alive."

Perpetua's eyes grew wide as saucers. "What?! You don't think...?"

"Shhhh!" Daniel stole a quick glance over his shoulder again before leaning in closer to her and whispering, "I don't know. But what if they're lying to us?"

Perpetua stared at him for a minute with her mouth hanging open before saying firmly, "I'm coming with you." Daniel had been expecting this type of reaction, he knew Perpetua well enough now to know that she had no fear, but he'd already resolved to say no. Although a part of him really wanted her to join him (the idea of heading willingly into the dungeons seemed almost suicidal; a companion would make the task less daunting) he couldn't risk allowing any harm to come to her. It was bad enough that George had been arrested; he couldn't stand to lose Perpetua too.

"No!" he said. "I'm going alone." Perpetua glared at him stubbornly and opened her mouth to argue but was interrupted when a loud bell suddenly began to toll.

"Oh no!" said Daniel. "Is that the afternoon bell already?!" Abruptly, he turned and ran toward the door. "Sister Anna will have my head if I'm not back in time for prayer!" Luckily, he managed to dart into the room and kneel quietly at the back before anyone noticed he was gone. Immediately he joined the others in praying.

"Our Father who art in heaven, hallowed be Thy name. Thy kingdom come. Thy will be done on earth, as it is in heaven. Give us today our daily bread, and deliver us from evil; for Thine is the power and the glory for ever. Amen." After more than forty days of living among early Christians, Daniel had grown accustomed to their prayer rituals and had even begun to draw comfort from them. Three times a day, no matter where he was, he stopped what he was doing and prayed the Our Father. First at nine o'clock, when the morning bell tolled, then again at noon, when the lunch bell tolled, and finally at three, when the afternoon bell tolled signaling all citizens to return to work. These were dark days, filled with danger and uncertainty, but each time he prayed he was given a renewed sense of hope and purpose.

That afternoon, while he prayed, he contemplated the task ahead. He knew that it would be dangerous, but ever since his talk with Pasicrates, when he'd learned the truth about George's ordeal in prison, he'd felt that he must see him. He needed to know that he was all right, but he was prepared for the worst. He had a nagging feeling that things weren't as they seemed, that really George was already dead and the emperor was just keeping the horrible truth from them all. If he wasn't dead, if he was in prison and all this time had been suffering torture... Daniel shuddered and tried not to think about it. But that wasn't all that was worrying him. What if George was dead and he, Daniel, was still here, trapped in 303 A.D.? What then? No, there was no other way. He would have to sneak into the prison and see for himself.

Prayer time ended, and all around him people rose to resume their chores. He squeezed his eyes tight and asked God for the strength to go through with his plan, then he too rose to his feet.

A little while later he peeked into the courtyard to see if Perpetua was still hanging laundry, but she was nowhere to be seen. He supposed that the bells had woken the twins.

For the next hour or so, he moved around in a kind of daze, mulling over the daunting task that he'd set out for himself. He was just wondering whether he should go and look for Perpetua, so that they could finish their discussion, when he accidentally stumbled upon her hurrying through the garden behind two naked toddlers. In one hand she clung to the skirt of her dress, which was hiked up above her knees, and in the other she carried two tiny, faded, white tunics. Her face was flushed. Before Daniel had a chance to muster out any words she shot past him and said matter-of-factly, "Don't even bother. I'm coming whether you like it or not!"

+

As luck would have it (or perhaps fate, or divine intervention), Anna allowed them to leave a little earlier than normal that afternoon. Although it had been a warm spring day, by the time they set out a damp chill had already begun to settle in on the city. They walked quickly, not daring to stop and warm themselves by one of the many fires that burned along the way. Normally they hurried straight home after work, to find Juliana waiting for them. Daniel wondered how she'd react when they didn't arrive home at their usual time. The thought of it made him feel uncomfortable with guilt, so he forced himself to think of something else. He tried focusing on the exotic assortment of people they passed; brown skinned women in colourful ankle-length silk dresses, and long haired men with bushy beards and belted tunics. He was trying not to stare at a crippled man hobbling past on a makeshift cane when he saw something that made him jump.

"Ahhh!" he yelled.

Perpetua stiffened and looked quickly from side to side for the source of his terror. "What is it?!" she cried. He pointed down a back alley toward the spot where a large rat had just disappeared.

"Did you see the size of that mouse?!" he asked, his voice about two octaves higher than usual.

"That wasn't a mouse," said Perpetua, relaxing. "It was a rat."

"A rat?!" repeated Daniel, scanning the surrounding area frantically, as though expecting others to suddenly jump out at him.

Perpetua looked at him funny. "Honestly," she said, "you're so weird. You act as though you've never seen one before."

"I haven't!" He insisted, but he could tell by the look on her face that she didn't believe him, so he hastily added, "There are no rats where I come from!"

Perpetua rolled her eyes. "Yeah, right," she muttered under her breath.

"I'm serious! There aren't!"

"Fine, fine, I believe you," she said, although it was clear from her tone that she didn't. A few minutes later she glanced sideways at him and was slightly irritated to find that he was still peering around himself nervously as they walked. "They're just rats, Daniel," she said, annoyed. "They're not going to hurt you."

"Not going to hurt me!? They're filthy creatures. They started the Black Plague, you know...killed thousands of people." He said this with his nose scrunched up in disdain, as though he'd just encountered something that smelled bad. He'd forgotten that the Black Plague, which killed more than two thirds of the population of Europe, didn't strike until the fourteenth century, but Perpetua didn't catch his slip up because during her time diseases and plagues posed a constant threat. Instead she rolled her eyes again.

"They're animals, Daniel, not people," she said. "You can't catch a plague from an animal."

"Oh yes you can!" he insisted.

"Yeah, right, and the world is round," she muttered.

"The world *is* round," he said in exasperation, "it's like I told you before, the world is round, and it floats in outer space along with eight other planets. No, wait a minute...I don't think Pluto's a planet anymore, so that makes seven other planets in our solar system."

Perpetua frowned. "How come Pluto's not a planet anymore?" she asked. "Did God destroy it?"

"What?! No!" he laughed. "No...it's just been changed from a planet to something else. I'm not sure why. I think scientists decided that they'd been wrong about it somehow."

"Oh," said Perpetua, clearly confused. "Well, I've never heard of it. I've always been told that there are only five planets, and the moon and the sun, of course. And I have *never* heard anyone say that the earth is round! That just doesn't make sense to me. The heavens are all up above us, moving around. They can't possibly be *under* us."

"They *are* under us!" said Daniel. "The earth is round, and it floats in space around the sun, along with all of the other planets. Jupiter, Mars…"

Perpetua grimaced. "Stop," she said uneasily.

"What?" he frowned. "What's the matter?"

"I just don't think we should be talking about this," she said, quickening her pace. "Jupiter and Mars are false gods. They don't inhabit the heavens."

"What?" said Daniel, comprehension slowly dawning on him. He'd never really thought about the names of the planets in that way before; he'd never associated them with the pagan gods. "No Perpetua. I know they're not gods. Those are just their names."

She kept walking and waved her hand at him, motioning for him to stop talking. "I don't think we should talk about it anymore," she breathed.

"All right, if you say so," said Daniel. He couldn't understand why she was being so superstitious. They were, after all, just names. He supposed that he'd given her too much information, that she just wasn't ready to know everything that he did. *Knowledge must be something that needs to be built upon,* he thought, *layer by layer.* He was walking along, thinking about how much the world has changed when all of a sudden Perpetua stopped and turned to face him.

"Daniel," she said, "where's God?"

His jaw dropped. Looking into her face he was horrified to see tears glistening in her eyes. "What?" he said stupidly.

"Where's God," she repeated, "and why does He keep letting the people I love get taken from me?" Daniel didn't know what to say, but he felt like this was one of those moments when he was expected to say something brilliant, or at least something that would make her feel better.

"I don't know," he said quietly. "I don't think anyone really knows…but I do know that I feel closer to Him now than I've ever felt before. He's here with us, Perpetua, I'm sure of it, and I imagine that when I go back home He'll come with me because…He's a part of me. He's here," he pressed his palm to his chest, "inside. Do you know what I mean?" He hoped that she understood his rambling.

She nodded. "Yes, I think I know what you mean. My mother used to say that when we welcome God into our hearts we become instruments of His peace." She sniffed and wiped her eyes with the back of her hand. "What do you think is going to happen to George?" she asked. Daniel avoided her gaze by staring at the ground. That was the question that he'd hoped she'd never ask.

"Daniel," she said suspiciously, "what is it? What are you not telling me?"

"Nothing," he lied and turned to go, but she grabbed him by the arm.

"Daniel, why are you here?" she persisted. "Are you an angel?" The question caught him off guard, and he looked at her quickly to see if she was joking. She wasn't. *Him? An angel?* He laughed at the absurdity of it.

"No!" he said. "Why would you think that?"

"I don't know. Pasicrates said that you were like an angel…that you were only going to be with us for a short time, and I thought that…you know…I was hoping that maybe you'd be able to help Uncle George." Daniel was overcome with pity. *Poor Perpetua.* But he also felt a rising sense of panic brought on by her words. *What was he doing here?* He'd asked himself that question a million times before. He turned abruptly and continued walking again in the direction of the prison.

"Come on," he said. "We don't have much time."

(XIX)

He was glad that Perpetua had insisted on joining him. Finding the prison proved to be much more difficult than he'd imagined. But after searching for almost an hour, and asking directions from a couple of dusty looking tradesmen dressed in ankle-length tunics and leather sandals who were packing away their tools at a busy construction site, they finally found their way.

They stood across the narrow street and stared nervously toward the entrance to where a group of soldiers stood gossiping and whistling at passing women. Daniel was telling Perpetua that he thought they should come up with a plan to get past the guards, something that involved one of them causing a distraction, but as usual, she had her own ideas.

"We can't just walk past them," he argued. "That'll never work."

"Yes we can," she said. "Watch." And before he could try and talk her out of it she was striding across the street straight toward the entrance. Cursing under his breath, he hurried after her.

They were just about to slide in past the distracted guards, when one of them turned and called out, "Hey! Where do you think you're going?" Daniel's stomach lurched. In an instant, the young soldier reached the spot

140 *St. George's Mysterious Cross*

where he and Perpetua stood frozen, waiting. He drew up in front of them, eyeing them suspiciously. He was tall and gangly, and his uniform was a little too snug. He had the look of someone who'd grown several inches overnight and was still trying to get used to his new body. Despite this, Daniel couldn't help but admire his appearance, the metal breastplate and helmet, dull and scuffed from repeated wear, the heavy red cloak, and most of all, the powerful sword that dangled at his side.

"What are you doing here?" he asked again. While Daniel struggled to find his voice, Perpetua began to plead tearfully.

"It's my uncle. He's in here somewhere, and I just want to see him one last time before he's…" She hid her face in her hands and sobbed.

The guard looked uncomfortable. "Well, I don't know…" he said uncertainly. "We've been given orders to not let anyone in." Daniel could tell by the tone of his voice that he could be persuaded. He was given new hope.

"We promise we won't be long," he said. "Just in and out."

The guard considered him for a moment. "Who's your uncle?" he asked.

Perpetua looked up, her face streaked with fresh tears. "Count George," she whispered. The guard opened his eyes wide. He bit his lip and glanced apprehensively over his shoulder toward the other guards, who were still busy catcalling at passing girls.

"Follow me then," he said, "but we'll have to be quick."

Daniel couldn't believe their luck. He stepped in line behind Perpetua and the young guard and followed them through the forbidding entrance and down a musty, narrow stairwell that seemed to have been carved right out of the earth. The lower they descended, the darker it got. When they reached the bottom and were about to pass through a doorway, he was struck by a disturbing thought.

Leaning forward he whispered in Perpetua's ear. "Do you think there are any rats in this place?" In response, she kicked the heel of her sandal into his shin. He winced and gingerly rubbed the spot where he'd been hit.

The guard led them through a dark, dingy passageway. Here there was no more daylight; the walls were lined with torches that flickered and sputtered as they passed. Daniel blinked into the darkness and peered from side to side. There was no sign of people, but he could hear voices in the next room. The smell had gotten worse; it was like a mixture of mildew, urine, sweat, and something else — something rotten. He fought the urge to turn and run back toward daylight and fresh air by taking several deep, calming breaths and reminding himself of why he was here. George. It was all about George.

When they turned the corner he was horrified to discover the source of the voices he'd heard. More than a dozen Christians were locked behind bars in the filthy confines of a long, narrow room, which ran the entire length of the corridor.[*] Daniel shook away unbidden thoughts of zoos and peered in tentatively. It was a depressing sight to behold: men and women of all ages, sitting spread out around the room, covered in grime from their time spent living, eating, sleeping, and praying together in squalor on the damp dirt floor. Several overflowing chamber pots were lined up against the wall, the stench of which was so

---

[*] Roman prisons weren't designed for rehabilitation, but were instead small, temporary holding cells, where the accused were kept while awaiting trial or execution.

overpowering that he had to cover his face and turn his head as he passed in order to avoid gagging.

As he followed Perpetua and the guard down the dim corridor, a thin, pale woman who'd been kneeling in prayer over the sleeping body of her sick brother, rose and stretched her filthy arm out through the bars. "Have mercy on us!" she pleaded.

Daniel shrunk away from her outstretched arm, appalled, but Perpetua stopped and reached out and touched her. "I pray for you often," she said bravely. "Don't be afraid. God loves you, and you'll soon be with Him. Remember us when you're in heaven; remember us and pray for us."

"I will child," wept the woman. "God bless you." And then another feeling overcame Daniel — guilt. He marveled at Perpetua's love. *She's used to this,* he told himself. *She's not from the future like I am. I've never been exposed to this kind of cruelty.* And then he remembered footage he'd once seen of the holocaust and was reminded that human cruelty is not just a thing of the distant past.

They stopped in front of a heavy wooden door, with a small, barred window. The guard glanced through it before turning the lock and pulling it open.

"Be quick," he said, moving aside to let them pass. Perpetua hesitated briefly and then took a deep breath and stepped into the cell, with Daniel following close on her heels.

It was darker than it had been in the main corridor, and the air was damp and stale. A single torch burned dimly in a bracket on the far wall. They paused just inside the doorway and peered uncertainly into the darkness of what appeared to be an empty room. Perpetua shivered involuntarily and leaned in closer to Daniel. Suddenly the door behind them swung shut with a bang, making them jump. Daniel spun around and tried the handle but, to his horror, found that it was locked. Just then, a low, hoarse voice called out to them from the depths of the room. "Who's there?"

Together, they swung around in the direction of the voice and for the first time, noticed a figure slumped on the floor in the corner. He sat with his back against the wall and his knees bent. His left wrist was strapped in a metal shackle and raised awkwardly above his head where it was chained to a hook on the wall. His ankles were also bound by shackles and chains. Perpetua leaned forward to try and see better.

"Un...Uncle George?" she stammered.

"Perpetua? Is that you?" returned the voice.

At once, Perpetua rushed forward and threw herself into her uncle's arms. "Thank God you're alive!" she sobbed, wrapping her arms tightly around his neck.

He winced at her touch. "Be careful," he breathed. She released him from her grasp and leaned back onto her haunches to get a better look at him. He was dirty and unshaven. The wound that Galerius had inflicted upon his cheek had long since healed but a long pink scar remained. There was a cut under one of his eyes, and the skin surrounding it was a multitude of colours — black, blue, green, yellow. He looked terrible, thin and weak, a mere shell of the man that he'd once been. Staring down at him, Daniel was overcome with pity. He had a burning desire to run to him, unchain him, and set him free.

"Are you hurt?" Perpetua asked softly. "Have they beaten you badly?"

"I'll be fine," he said reassuringly. "Let me have a look at you." Gingerly, he shifted his body into a more upright position and cupped her face with his chained hand. "It's so nice to see you," he began, then, as though suddenly remembering where they were, he dropped his hand and frowned. "You shouldn't be here," he said hoarsely. "Does anyone know you've come?"

Perpetua and Daniel looked at one another guiltily. "No," said Perpetua, "but we just had to see you. We were worried." Before George could open his mouth to scold her, she wrapped her arms around him again, this time more gently.

Daniel hung back and watched. He was relieved to see that George was still alive, but Deacon Adrian's foreboding words kept running through his mind. *They're torturing him...doing every horrific thing imaginable to make him change his mind!* His eyes swept over George's body as he searched for any signs of torture. With a sickening feeling he noticed that his unchained arm wasn't wrapped around Perpetua, as would be expected, but instead hung limp and useless at his side. He frowned and was about to take a step closer when Perpetua suddenly withdrew her embrace.

"Your back," she said in a puzzled voice, "it's wet..." She looked down at her hands and gasped. They were sticky with blood.

Daniel rushed forward. Before George could protest, he and Perpetua had yanked aside his filthy tunic to reveal a back, torn and bloody with open sores and deep gashes. He winced when they touched his right arm, which hung at an odd angle. Perpetua recoiled in horror and put her hands to her mouth in a silent scream.

"What have they done to you!" gasped Daniel. Nothing could have prepared him for this moment. No stories, poems, or paintings could ever succeed in describing the agony of George's torture nor the pain which pierced Daniel's heart as he stared, outraged at his wounded body. He stumbled backwards, anger coursing through his veins. "It's not fair!" he shouted, tears welling up in his eyes and spilling over onto his cheeks. He wiped them away impatiently and spun around, kicking the nearest wall as hard as he could. It felt good to let out some of the frustration that he'd been keeping bottled up for so long. He was sick of living in fear, sick of being bullied. "I hate them!" he yelled. "All of them! I'll..."

"Stop!" commanded George. "Please...no more..." Despite his weak and injured body, he'd managed to pull himself to his feet and was now leaning heavily against the wall, staring over at Daniel with a worried expression on his pale face. "I know it's difficult, but we mustn't let them get to us," he pleaded. "We mustn't give in to the hatred. If we do they'll have won. Don't you see? There will be no end."

"What can we do, Uncle?" sobbed Perpetua as she tried to wipe the blood from her hands. "Surely there must be something? We can't just sit back and let them destroy us."

"They won't destroy us, Pet, as long as we remain faithful to our Lord Jesus Christ. Come here," he beckoned her forward and gently pulled her head into his chest with his shackled hand.

Daniel folded his arms up over his head and pressed his forehead into the cool wall. George's words had done nothing to diminish his anger. Visions kept flashing across his mind — the pile of rubble that used to be the cathedral, soldiers tossing holy book after holy book into a great flaming fire, a frightened woman desperately begging for mercy, George's body, broken and bloody... So much violence and suffering...and for what!? For believing in God and wanting to worship him!? Consumed with anger, he spun around and faced George.

"So that's it?" he said, his voice shaking with suppressed rage. "We do nothing?"

"Not nothing," said George calmly. "We pray." Daniel snorted contemptuously. Pray?! This was the great soldier's solution?! Innocent people are being murdered and he wants to pray?! Daniel glared at George in frustration. He wanted to shake him, to make him understand that action was what was needed, not prayer!

"I thought you were a soldier!" he said viciously. George stiffened as though he'd been slapped in the face. Daniel knew instantly that he'd crossed the line, that his words had been mean and hateful, but he didn't care, he wanted to give in to the hatred, to spread it around.

"I am a soldier," said George evenly.

"Then why aren't you fighting!" hollered Daniel. George's hand fell away from Perpetua, and he took a step toward Daniel. His eyes blazed, and his body seemed to have miraculously grown back to its original splendour.

"You may not have noticed," he began quietly, through clenched teeth, and then, in a powerful torrent of unbridled fury and tugging fiercely at his chains he shouted, "I'm chained to a goddamn wall!"

Daniel and Perpetua flinched and backed away, but almost the instant that it had happened, it was over. Once again, George was leaning into the wall, weak and exhausted. He stared over at the two kids, remorse etched into his young, bruised face.

"I'm sorry," he whispered, almost inaudibly, "truly, I…" Shamefully, he covered his face with his chained hand. An uncomfortable tension filled the room. Daniel felt numb. His anger had dissipated as suddenly and thoroughly as if he'd been doused in a bucket of ice water.

After several long moments of silence, Perpetua moved forward and wrapped her arms comfortingly around George's waist. He kissed the top of her head, welcoming her touch. Daniel's eyes burned. He blinked and focused his gaze on an indecipherable etching in the far wall, no doubt left as the final will and testament of a previous prisoner.

"This isn't easy for me, Daniel," said George. "It may not seem like it to you, but I am fighting, the most difficult battle of my life. I've laid down my sword and given myself over to the Lord. Now I fight according to His will."

"His will?" Daniel whispered incomprehensibly.

George nodded. "Yes, Daniel," he said firmly, "*His* will. Never underestimate the power of peaceful action."

Daniel nodded. "I'm sorry," he whispered, "I..." His voice broke.

George nodded in understanding, drew Perpetua into a tight embrace and closed his eyes. "Look," he said, "you asked if there was something that you could do for me. Well, there is."

Perpetua looked up into his face. "What is it?" she asked. "Anything."

"Pray for me," he said hoarsely. Fresh tears streamed down Perpetua's cheeks, and she pressed her face into his chest. Daniel held his breath trying not to cry. "Ask God to be merciful when he judges me."

"Of course, uncle," sobbed Perpetua, "but surely you don't need us to. You're a saint."

"I'm not perfect, Pet," he whispered. "War..." His voice broke. "Please, promise me you'll pray for me."

(XX)

Neither of them spoke much on the journey home. In his mind, Daniel kept replaying everything that had happened at the prison. No matter how much he tried, he couldn't shake away the memory of George's body, broken and bruised. He berated himself for having gone at all. *I feel worse now than I did before I went. What could I possibly have been thinking? Was I so deluded as to think that I'd be able to rescue him? Still, at least now I know for sure that he's still alive, that's something…maybe there is still hope…* And so it went.

As they made their way up the rickety, wooden stairs to the apartment, Daniel's stomach churned. He prayed that they weren't too late for supper. It had already been a long day; he didn't think that he could stand another scene.

When they walked through the door Pasicrates was sitting in a chair, reading. The familiar sound of dishes clattering as they were being washed emanated from the kitchen.

Too late, thought Daniel dismally.

Pasicrates looked up at them as they entered. "Peace," he said.

Daniel relaxed a little. "Peace," replied he and Perpetua in unison.

"May I ask where you've been?" said Pasicrates, not unkindly.

Daniel and Perpetua glanced sideways at each other. This time is was Daniel who spoke up. "We went to see George." He looked down at his dusty sandals and held his breath, waiting for an onslaught, but none came. Instead, Pasicrates set aside his scroll.

"And how was he?" he asked. Daniel shrugged his shoulders and continued to stare down at his feet. He wouldn't allow himself to cry, not in front of Pasicrates. He concentrated on his toenails, which he noticed needed to be trimmed.

"May I go and help Juliana in the kitchen?" asked Perpetua quietly from somewhere at his side. Pasicrates nodded his approval.

Daniel continued to stare down at his feet. After a few moments, Pasicrates spoke.

"Go and eat, brother, and when you've finished, I have something for you to read." Relieved, Daniel swung around and sped off toward the kitchen.

After devouring the meal that Juliana had set aside for him (unleavened bread and a bowl of lentil soup that had grown cold in his tardiness) he returned to the sitting room to do his reading. Pasicrates, who hadn't moved from his spot, looked up when he walked in.

"Go and fetch Perpetua," he said. "She needs to study too."

Daniel spun around again and headed back the way he'd come. He found Perpetua standing in the middle of the kitchen talking to Juliana. She held a stationary broom in one hand, and there were tears sliding down her cheeks. Juliana was patting her comfortingly on the back. The two of them looked up when he entered.

"Sorry," he said, "but Pasicrates wants you to come and work on your studies."

Perpetua wiped her eyes and turned back to her sweeping. "Tell him I'm busy," she said.

Daniel shook his head. "No, Perpetua, you'd better come. I don't think any of your excuses are going to work tonight."

A few minutes later, the two of them were seated in the main room, near the light of an open window shutter. A cool breeze blew in, causing Daniel to shiver slightly. He pulled a heavy blanket around his shoulders and clutched his hot apple tea tightly between his two hands in an effort to warm them.

With the arrival of spring, the days had grown longer, allowing he and Perpetua more time in the evening to work on their studies. Candles and fuel were expensive luxuries and were not normally burned late into the night, which meant that on a typical evening, as soon as the sun set and darkness closed in, they would call it a day. Unlike at home in the twenty first century, where Daniel would often stay up well past dark reading or playing on the computer, here his daily routines were guided by the natural rhythms of the world.

Pasicrates handed the two of them their reading, Daniel a scroll and Perpetua a book bound in a hard, wooden cover. With the exception of a few small nicks and scratches, the cover of the book was smooth and completely bare. Daniel had never seen it before. He stared over at it curiously, wondering what it was.

After muttering something under her breath about time being wasted, Perpetua reached for the nearest blanket, spread it out on the floor, and plopped down on top of it.

"Be extra careful with that codex, Perpetua," cautioned Pasicrates. "The binding is broken. I meant to fix it earlier today."

"What is it?" asked Daniel. "The cover is bare."

"The Gospel of Matthew," explained Pasicrates. "Sometimes discretion is the surest path to survival."

Daniel nodded. He knew what Pasicrates meant. The blank cover was a way of disguising the book and keeping it from being burned. He wondered how old it was. *Pretty old, I think. I suppose Christians have always been persecuted, ever since the beginning, when Christ himself was crucified. Wasn't Saint Peter crucified upside down?* He couldn't remember for sure. *And the rest of the apostles? How did they die?** Probably not from natural causes.* He shook the thought from his mind and turned his attention to the scroll that Pasicrates had given him. In thin, curvy letters across the top was written:

These are the secret sayings that the living Jesus spoke and Didymos Judas Thomas recorded.

He blinked. *Secret sayings?* "What is this?" he asked.

"The Gospel of Thomas**," said Pasicrates, settling into his chair. "Are you not familiar with it?"

---

* Popular belief holds that St. Peter was crucified upside down, St. Andrew and St. Philip were crucified, St. Matthew and St. Thomas were stabbed with a spear, St. Bartholomew was flayed and beheaded, St. John died of natural causes, St. James (the first apostle to be martyred) died by the sword, St. Simon was sawed in two, St. Jude and St. Matthias were killed with a halberd, and St. James the Less was either stoned or clubbed to death.

** The Gospel of Thomas is a list of 114 sayings attributed to Jesus. It was discovered in Egypt in 1945, among a collection of other non-canonical early Christian writings (writings that were not included in the Bible). These writings were probably hidden in the 4th century when they were deemed heretical (not accepted by the Church). There are two main reasons why the Gospel of Thomas was not canonized: the author is unknown (although it bears his name, it does not appear to have been written by the apostle Thomas), and it contains traces of Gnosticism (the belief that salvation is attained through knowledge rather than by faith and good works).

Daniel shook his head. "No. I'd never even heard of it before I came here." His mind returned to the day he'd arrived, on the eve of the Festival of Terminalia when the cathedral had been destroyed. He remembered sitting in this very room and listening to everyone discuss the possibility of a persecution. George had asked whether or not the Gospel of Thomas had been burned, and Bishop Anthimus had said that it was.

"I thought that this was destroyed along with the cathedral," he said.

"Not this one," said Pasicrates. "It's our own copy. Actually, it belongs to Perpetua," his eyes flickered to where she lay sprawled out, reading. "It was her mother's." Daniel ran his finger over the curvy letters. The idea that Perpetua's mother had once sat and read this very same scroll sent chills down his spine. With a renewed sense of interest, he settled back in his chair and began to read.

He was part way down the page when there was a knock at the front door. Pasicrates rose abruptly and pressed his finger to his lips. Daniel and Perpetua froze, their eyes focused on the door. The knocking came again, this time in a definite rhythmic sequence; three slow knocks, followed by a long pause and three quick tap, tap, taps. Daniel relaxed a little; it was definitely the secret knock. Perpetua began to rise noisily to her feet, but Pasicrates scowled and gestured for her to remain still. It was probably someone from the Church bringing them news, or perhaps a woman with her kids, tearful and in distress because her husband had disappeared. That had happened before. But there was always the chance that it was the soldiers themselves. These were dangerous times, and you could never be too careful.

As the three of them waited in silence, Pasicrates motioned for Daniel to gather the scriptures together and take them into the other room. Quickly and quietly, he did as he was told. Once inside his room, he stood with his back against the door and stared wildly around for a place to hide them. *The person at the door is probably someone we know,* he reasoned, *but what if it's not? What if someone gave away the secret knock while they were being tortured?* His mind raced, and his eyes frantically swept the room. Other than the bed, it was pretty much empty. Without wasting any more time, he rushed toward the mattress, heaved up one of its corners and tried sliding the scriptures underneath. The mattress was stuffed with straw making it incredibly heavy. In an effort to raise the corner higher, he wedged his knee under it, but in doing so, lost his grip on the codex. With a heavy clunk, it tumbled to the floor and fell open. Loose pages scattered at his feet. Cursing softly under his breath he paused to listen; thankfully, there was still no sound coming from the other room. Hurriedly, he gathered together all of the loose papers and slid them carefully under the mattress. He knew that this was probably the most pathetic hiding place in the Empire; he'd really only chosen it out of sheer desperation. If it were soldiers at the door, and if they'd come to search for sacred writings, he was almost certain that they'd look under all of the beds. He remembered only too well the searches that had taken place at the orphanage. He was considering prying open one of the floorboards when there was a knock at his door.

"Daniel," said Pasicrates, his voice sounding muffled through the door, "it's safe to come out." Daniel opened his bedroom door and peeked out. Juliana, Perpetua, and

Pasicrates were all standing in the centre of the room, looking at him as though someone had died. His stomach dropped.

"What is it?" he asked.

"We've just received word," said Pasicrates, "George's hearing has been set…for tomorrow morning."

"What?!" he looked at Perpetua and knew instantly that it was true. Her face was pale, her lip trembling.

"I'm afraid that I can't stay," said Pasicrates, reaching for his cloak. "You'll be safe here with Juliana. Oh, and Daniel," he said as he headed for the door, "could you please take the scriptures out from under the mattress and hide them in their secret spot, under the floorboard in the kitchen."

Daniel's mouth fell open. "How…?"

Pasicrates smiled and winked before pulling the door shut behind him.

(XXI)

Soon after Pasicrates' departure, Daniel said his good nights and crawled into bed. The knowledge that George would soon be forced to stand before a judge made him feel sick with grief. Despite his anxiety, he was exhausted and sleep soon overtook him...

He was walking down a busy street with his best friend Steve. It was dusk, that brief moment between day and night, and the city was pulsating with life. Shiny sports cars and SUVs zoomed past, music blaring from their open windows. The sidewalks were bustling with people in designer jeans and tailored suits who all seemed in a hurry to get somewhere. Every now and then, one of them would break from the tide and disappear, empty handed, into a brightly lit shop, only to re-emerge several minutes later, their arms laden with colourful plastic bags emblazoned with names like "Trinkets and Things" and "Gotta Have It." They passed by a series of chic outdoor cafes and noisy taverns, finally stopping in front of a restaurant. The neon sign overhead read, "Frank's Fast Food."

Daniel's stomach growled in anticipation as he swung open the front door and stepped inside. The place was hopping. He followed Steve across the expansive dining room, humming along contentedly with the catchy commercial jingle blaring from the overhead TV screens. Stylish men and women were scattered throughout, laughing as they swapped stories and sipped on chocolate lattes and Bloody Marys. Clearly this was the place to be. Three long tables had been pushed together at the back of the room and were surrounded by a rowdy group of kids, all the same age as Daniel. He and Steve slid into the two empty chairs that had been reserved for them and joined in the fun. Before long, the pizza and drinks arrived. Daniel couldn't remember ever tasting anything so good.

He was tucking away his fourth slice and listening to a particularly funny joke when something brushed his elbow. Looking up, he was startled to find a tall, slim man with long dark hair and a beard that was beginning to go grey standing by his side, gazing down at him thoughtfully, and holding out an envelope. He recognized him from somewhere but couldn't quite remember where.

"You mustn't forget to do your reading, brother," said the man. Daniel reached for the envelope, opened it, and read:

Where is God?

He gasped and threw his hand to his neck. What am I doing here, he wondered, panic stricken, and what's happened to my cross?!

The room disappeared, and he was engulfed in a white, swirling mist. Then the mist rose, and he was standing alone, on the edge of a rocky outcropping. Green pastures stretched out before him, as far as the eye could see, while above him white puffy clouds floated in a sparkling blue sky. Quickly, he turned and scanned the nearby boulders, searching, certain that what he was looking for was nearby. He soon spotted an opening. Every nerve in his body was taut as he approached the mouth of the cave. Once at the entrance he peered inside and listened. A slow, raspy sound emanated from the darkness and echoed menacingly off the walls. He knew that the beast was sleeping — he didn't know how he knew it, but he did — and that even while it slept, it guarded his prize jealously. But it was his! And he must have it!

Emboldened, he hastened into the cave and crept toward the dragon. The stench was overpowering, but still he snuck forward, until he was crouched directly in front of the great winged creature, close enough to touch it. And there it was, his cross, just inches away, shiny and glistening like a pearl. He stretched out his hand and slowly...slowly...reached for it. Hardly daring to breathe, he wrapped his fingers gently around the chain and clutched the cross tightly in his fist. He could feel the warm breath of the dragon on the back of his hand. His face was so close to the beasts that he could clearly make out each scale along its snout, could see its eyes flicker beneath their lids. A bead of sweat trickled down the side of his face as he quietly began backing his way out of the lair. Just as he thought that he was home free, the dragon's cat like eyes suddenly flicked open and stared directly into his. Terrorized, he turned and scrambled through the opening, cutting one of his knees on a jagged rock in the process. But he felt no pain, only fear, as he ran, as fast as his legs would carry him, away from that cave, toward home! He heard the awful roar of the beast behind him and felt a blast of heat on the back of his neck. And then in the distance he saw him, George, galloping toward him on his steed. At last!

He awoke with a start, his heart pounding in his chest, and tried to cling to the dream. But like a castle made of sand, it soon dissolved, and he was left with nothing more than a lingering feeling of nervousness and anticipation. Turning over onto his back, he let his thoughts drift to George and wondered if he too was lying awake, staring up at the ceiling and dreading the day ahead.

Gradually, the long, narrow gap surrounding his window shutters turned from black to a soft shade of gold, and the birds began to chirp. Shivering, he crawled out of bed and knelt on the hard floor with his head bowed. Yesterday he'd promised George that he'd pray for him, and he wasn't about to break that promise. He closed his eyes and raised his right hand to his forehead. *In the name of the Father, and of the Son, and of the Holy Spirit.* He prayed for a longtime, until he could hear movements from within the apartment and finally someone knocking on his door.

"Who is it?" he said, rising to his feet. His legs were cramped. The door opened a crack, and Perpetua peeked in.

"It's me," she said. "Juliana wants you to come and eat something before we go."

"Thanks," he said, "tell her I'll be out in a minute." He changed into his daytime tunic and slipped into his sandals before heading into the kitchen. Perpetua was standing next to the warm brazier, staring absent-mindedly at the smoldering embers and munching on a slice of pan-fried cornbread. Juliana was busy sweeping what appeared to be a perfectly clean floor. She looked up at him and smiled when he entered. Her eyes were puffy and red.

"Help yourself to some breakfast," she said, motioning to a plate, which held two slices of bread. "Take them both. The rest of us won't be eating today. 'Tis a day of fasting."

Daniel's stomach fluttered uneasily. "I'm not hungry," he said. "I think I'd rather fast today too."

"Nonsense," said Juliana, "you need the nourishment, you're a growing boy. Eat." In order to appease her, he reached for a slice and took a small bite. His mouth was dry, and he was pouring himself a cup of water to help wash it down when Deacon Adrian appeared in the doorway, his curly black hair unkempt and dark circles under his eyes.

"We'll need to leave soon," he announced hoarsely. "By the sounds of it, more than half the city will be turning up for the hearing. The emperor himself will be there."

Perpetua gasped. "The emperor?!" she exclaimed. "Do you think we'll get to see him?"

Deacon Adrian shrugged. "Perhaps," he said carelessly. "Finish your meal quickly or I fear that by the time we get there the crowd will be so thick that we won't get anywhere near the basilica."

(XXII)

The air was cool as they set out, but just above the horizon a golden sun glowed in a cloudless sky promising another warm afternoon. Daniel pulled his hands up into his sleeves for warmth and fell in line behind the others. Even at this early hour, the streets had begun to bustle with activity. As they wound their way through the city toward the basilica, they were joined by many of their Christian brothers and sisters who were also on their way to the hearing, and soon Daniel found himself being carried along at the centre of a large group. While he walked, he listened to bits and pieces of the conversations going on around him.

"The emperor is wasting his time," the man in front of him grumbled to Deacon Adrian whose somber eyes remained fixed on the road ahead. "He knows as well as we do that George will never offer a sacrifice to the Roman gods. Lord knows he's tried. 'Tis a miracle that he's still alive."

"Yes," sniffed the man's wife, wiping her tears with a small, white cloth, "truly a miracle."

The man squeezed her hand comfortingly. "Speaking of the emperor," he continued, "I'm surprised he'll be present. What do you make of it?"

Deacon Adrian shrugged. "I'm only a man," he said sarcastically. "How should I know why the gods do the things they do."

The man threw back his head in bitter laughter. "Yes, well, you can be sure of one thing," he growled, "he won't be pleased with George's actions today. You mark my words, before this is over, the streets will be painted in the blood of the martyrs." Daniel's stomach churned nervously. He looked over at Perpetua, and their eyes met. From the look on her face it was clear that she too had heard the man's awful prediction and was sickened by it.

In an effort to calm her fears, he leaned over and whispered, "Don't listen to them. They've no idea how the hearing's going to turn out. Remember what Pasicrates told us, we must never lose hope." But even as he spoke, he realized that his words were as much for himself as they were for her.

Soon the streets became even more crowded. Daniel was just beginning to wonder how much farther they had to go when the tall white statue of Emperor Diocletian loomed overhead, signaling the entrance to the forum. They were halfway across the square when Daniel spotted a big, fat man in a toga, standing on a raised platform and speaking in a booming voice. He was bald and clean-shaven, and in his hand he held a long scroll from which he read the official news of the day, something about the rising price of figs and the daily bread quota. Daniel plodded on, listening without interest until the man's words made him stop in his tracks.

"George of Lydda, ex-Tribune of the Imperial Guard, shall be tried this morning in the basilica, for refusing to make a public sacrifice to the gods" he hollered. "Lord and Master, Gaius Aurelius Valerius Diocletianus, shall oversee the trial. No actors, workmen, slaves, or prostitutes shall be permitted entry." Daniel was shoved from behind as the crowd pressed in on him. He resumed walking and soon the orator's voice was swallowed up by the noise of the surrounding crowd.

When they reached the marble stairs to the basilica, Pasicrates turned to face Daniel and Perpetua. "We're going to head inside now and try to find a good spot from which to watch the proceedings," he said. "It's going to be crowded, so be sure to stay close." Perpetua grabbed onto Daniel's hand, and he pulled her along after him as they squeezed their way up the stairs. At the top, dozens of guards stood watch, flexing their muscles and flaunting their swords. Daniel stared down at the ground and held his breath as he walked past them through the great front doors and into the basilica. Once safely inside, he looked up and gazed around himself in wonder.

Never in his life had he been inside such a magnificent building. The ceilings soared high above his head in glorious arches and beneath his feet the floors were adorned in colourful mosaics of various gods and goddesses. They climbed a wide staircase, which led to an upper balcony where many people had already begun to gather. Daniel recognized some of the faces from Mass; although their churches had all been destroyed, the faithful had continued to meet secretly in private homes where they would read from Scripture and share in the Eucharistic meal. As they worked their way through the crowd, Pasicrates stopped and greeted many of them the Christian way, with a kiss on the cheek. Finally they found a spot tucked away in a corner, next to an old friend of Pasicrates. While the two men talked, Daniel pulled off his cloak, dropped it onto the floor, and plunked himself down on top of it. It wasn't as noisy up here, but it was hot and stuffy. Perpetua sat down beside him, cross-legged, so that only her sandals peeked out from beneath the folds of her long dress, and stared down at the floor, picking absentmindedly at a loose string on one of her sandals. Daniel had never seen her so quiet and withdrawn. He wished he could think of something to cheer her up.

"I guess we'll know soon enough," he said. She nodded. Then he realized, with a pang, that she'd probably been through this before.

"Did your parents have a hearing too?" he asked. Again, she nodded. He wanted to ask her more but decided against it. She was obviously in no mood to discuss it. And anyway, he knew how that hearing had ended, and it wasn't pleasant.

All at once the chatter of the crowd died down, and people began clambering to their feet. Daniel and Perpetua jumped up in unison, both anxious to catch a glimpse of George, but it was no use, no matter which way they turned their view was obstructed by the hoard of spectators gathered in front of them. Then a booming voice from somewhere up ahead called out a series of indistinguishable words, and the room fell absolutely still and silent. The emperor had arrived. Daniel didn't need to be told; he knew it instinctively, could read it on the faces of those standing around him, which all bore the same look of awe, wonder, and dreadful anticipation. Spurred on by anxiety and an overwhelming desire to see George, Daniel peered frantically between the two men in front of him, searching for an opening, and spotted the balcony railing, several feet ahead. Dozens of people were already pressed up against it, but he felt certain that if he could somehow manage to squirm his way through the crowd, he'd be able to squeeze in among them. He nudged Perpetua, signaling for her to follow. As they elbowed their way forward, a longhaired, bushy-faced Christian man turned on them in annoyance, but when he recognized who they were, his expression softened and he stepped aside to let them pass. Finally, after much shoving and grumbling, they reached the balcony's edge, where they crammed themselves in among the other onlookers and gazed down with a bird's eye view at the main floor of the basilica and the hearing, which was now in progress.

The room was enormous, with high arched ceilings above, and row upon row of finely-dressed spectators below, all kneeling and facing the same direction, their heads bowed in servitude. A wide aisle cut down the centre of the room and was bordered on either side by two lines of tall white colonnades.

At the front, there was a raised area, like an altar, and three golden thrones on which sat Emperor Diocletian, Galerius Caesar, and the governor. On the largest and most central throne, clothed in the imperial purple cloak, a jewel encrusted crown, and pointy shoes trimmed in sparkling rubies and sapphires, Diocletian gazed majestically out over his subjects. Next to him, in a much less ornate throne, Galerius was busy whispering instructions into the ear of one of his servants. Daniel surveyed him with loathing before moving his eyes to the other man on Diocletian's left, the governor. He was the one who would normally oversee this type of proceeding. Although, like Diocletian and Galerius, he too was dressed in rich robes, he somehow came across as less showy, more business like. Several dozen officials were seated along the fringes, scribbling notes onto wax tablets and scanning scrolls through shrewd eyes. Stationed in a wide semi-circle behind the emperor, as well as all along the periphery of the room, were the Imperial Guards.

Daniel's eyes swept over the scene and soon rested on George, bowed down prostrate on the floor before Diocletian and flanked by two tall soldiers. He looked different than he had the last time that Daniel had seen him. Better. The shackles and chains were gone. His ragged beard and filthy, blood-soaked tunic were also gone. On the surface, he was once again young, strong, and handsome. Most of his wounds, which had been carefully cleaned and bandaged by the emperor's servants, were now hidden from view beneath a crisp white tunic — most, but not all — no amount of make-up could completely mask his bruised eye, and, unlike his left arm, his right wasn't stretched out in front of his body but instead hung limp at his side.

After everyone had settled back into their seats, the governor rose and moved forward. George's guards pulled him to his feet before taking two synchronized steps backwards, away from him, leaving him to stand alone before his judges.

"All citizens are required, by law, to offer a public sacrifice to the gods," stated the governor severely. "Come up then and sacrifice, lest you die an evil death."* The audience was dead quiet, every eye in the room fixed on George's young, bruised face. When he finally spoke, his jaw was set, his expression calm.

"There is only one God," he said clearly, "the maker and creator of all things." The governor scowled and moved to speak again but was stopped by Diocletian, who raised his hand, motioning for him to remain silent. Obediently, the governor bowed and retreated backwards into the shadows. Daniel gripped more tightly to the balcony railing and leaned forward, his heart beating rapidly.

---

* (p 99 Acts of SG)

"The law clearly states that Christianity is forbidden," roared the emperor from his throne. "Are you going to stand there, before all of these witnesses and continue to defy the orders of your Lord and Master?"

"I have but one Lord and Master," replied George. "His name is Jesus Christ, and *His* law forbids the worship of false gods." The crowd let out a collective gasp and broke out in excited whispers and murmurs.

From somewhere beyond Daniel's line of vision, a man stood and shouted, "God bless you, George!" If George heard him, he didn't betray it, but the emperor shot to his feet, his face contorted in rage.

"Silence!" he commanded. The imperial soldiers rushed forward as others also began to rise up and shout out in defiance.

"I too am a Christian!" yelled one.

"I will worship none but the One True God!" yelled another. Daniel watched in horror as the soldiers swarmed through the crowd and closed in on these zealots, beating them down mercilessly before dragging them away. Throughout it all, George never once looked back, knowing that to do so would risk opening the floodgates to unwanted feelings—anger, resentment, vengeance. He closed his eyes in an effort to shut out the screams and reminded himself of his task, and of the need to stay calm, focused. Infuriated by his meekness, one of his guards moved towards him and lashed out, brutally striking him across his lame arm. The pain was too much. No longer able to bear it George sank to his knees and cried out in agony for God's loving mercy.

Within minutes, the room was once again subdued. With the exception of the soldiers, Diocletian was now the only person left standing. Enraged, he glared down at

George's kneeling figure, his chest heaving with fury, and George knew that the moment that Diocletian had tried so hard to avoid had finally come.

"You leave me no choice," snarled the emperor, "but to find you guilty, and to sentence you to death." Stricken with grief, Perpetua slumped forward and buried her sobbing face in her lap. Daniel watched, as though from a great distance, as the frail old woman next to him reached out her crooked hand and placed it soothingly on Perpetua's trembling back. "He shall find glory in the Lord, child," she whispered. He was barely aware of the audience rising momentarily and of the emperor storming from the room, his long purple robe trailing in his wake. The crowd was subdued. There were no more cries of Christ's love, no more shouts. Some were stricken into silence out of fear, others smug glee. It was hard to know what each person was thinking, to show sorrow would be to risk death.

Galerius sat in silence, gazing out over the crowd. Daniel had the distinct impression that he was enjoying this, was drinking it in. Eventually his eyes came to rest on George kneeling submissively before him, and his mouth twisted into a wicked smile.

"George of Lydda," he sneered, "you are hereby sentenced to death by beheading. I see no point in delaying this any further. The sentence shall be carried out forthwith. On this, the ninth of the Calends of May, you shall be taken beyond the defensive wall where the governor shall oversee your execution." A wave of shock rippled through the audience. Galerius smiled. He loved the power. At that moment he felt victorious. Triumphant! But then George boldly raised his eyes and looked up into his face, and in George's eyes there was no fear, and Galerius's fleeting moment of victory was tarnished by doubt. He thrust out his lower jaw and clenched his fists in anger. For several long moments they stared at one another, Galerius with hatred, George pity, and then Galerius rose and stormed from the room.

Daniel closed his eyes and clenched his cross so tightly in his fist that his hand ached. Eventually someone tapped him gently on the shoulder.

"We must go now," urged Pasicrates. "Come, it is almost finished."

(XXIII)

Daniel followed the noisy crowd down the stairs and out into the blazing sunlight. Shielding his eyes against the sun, he stopped and gazed out over the forum at the long line of people heading off in the direction of the main gates, beyond which George would soon be executed. Juliana was up ahead, with her arm wrapped around Perpetua, and Pasicrates was looking back and waving him forward. He hesitated, wondering what would happen if he simply refused to go. Would the execution go on without him, or was his presence somehow required? Hoping, once again, that it was all just a bad dream sparked by a storybook about a brave knight battling an evil dragon, he pinched himself in the leg, but the scene before him remained unchanged. The ancient city continued to beckon him forward.

A warm breeze kissed his face. Spring was in full bloom now; soft pink flowers blossomed on fruit trees, and birds sang of hope and new life. Daniel stared down at the bustling city, the rich and the destitute, the golden litters and overburdened mules, the towering, white temples and decrepit shacks…. This was real but it wasn't his reality…or was it?

His stomach writhed and churned nervously. He wondered how George felt, knowing that soon… *No!* He shook his head stubbornly, still refusing to believe that it was true. He would never give up hope, not until it was over! Before heading down the stairs, he squared his shoulders and took a deep breath, resolving that he'd find a way to keep George alive, even if it was the last thing he did.

As they traveled through the city, those nearest to him began to sing a slow and mournful psalm, and soon many others had joined in. Daniel walked quietly behind Pasicrates and listened.

O God, you are my God,
I seek you,
my soul thirsts for you;
my flesh faints for you,
as in a dry and weary land where there is no water.
So I have looked upon you in the sanctuary,
beholding your power and glory.
Because your steadfast love is better than life,
my lips will praise you.
So I will bless you as long as I live;
I will lift up my hands and call on your name.
My soul is satisfied as with a rich feast,
and my mouth praises you with joyful lips.

When I think of you on my bed,
and meditate on you in the watches of the night;
for you have been my help,
and in the shadow of your wings I sing for joy.
My soul clings to you;
your right hand upholds me.

But those who seek to destroy my life
shall go down into the depths of the earth;
they shall be given over to the power of the sword;
They shall be a prey for jackals.

But the king shall rejoice in God;
all who swear by him shall exult,
for the mouths of liars will be stopped.
Psalm 63 (NJB)

The singing petered off as they approached the high, arched, mortar and stone gate to the city and the dozens of guards stationed there. The last time that Daniel had passed by this way George had accompanied him. He remembered it as though it were yesterday. He'd quaked at the sight of the soldiers, and George had drawn-up alongside him and said reassuringly, "Don't worry, everything will work out." Those had been his exact words. *Well he was wrong wasn't he?* thought Daniel, bitterly. *Everything hasn't worked out. He's about to be killed, and me, I'm still trapped.*

Soon the looming wall blotted out the overhead sun, and he stared down, self-consciously, at the ground before him. In the distance there was laughter and people talking and calling out to one another, but in the shadow of the wall, no one dared speak. Tension filled the air. Daniel could feel the eyes of the guards boring down on him, but he wasn't afraid anymore. He still found them intimidating, only a fool wouldn't, but over the weeks he'd grown accustomed to their presence. He'd learned that the best way to stay out of trouble was to just keep your head down and mind your own business; ignore them and they'll go away. *No,* said a voice inside of him, *no, that's not right. Ignoring them won't make them go away. They'll just keep at it and at it. Without people like George, willing to stand up to them, they'll never stop.* He thought of the news reports; they were always the same. Child slavery in Asia, bombings in the Middle East, children starving in Africa, and there was that grade ten girl who'd been picked on for so long that she'd finally taken her own life. And Ralph, the bus bully... They never stopped until someone was brave enough to step forward and tell them to. He realized now that it was the same all over, that some things never change, and he was struck with a thought: *What would the world be like without people like George? Would anyone stand up for the weak and defenseless?* Emboldened, he raised his head and looked up into the eyes of his oppressor. He was startled to find in them not anger or hatred but shame and something else — was it fear? It was a fleeting moment; soon the soldier had looked away and Daniel was once again out in the open, blinking under the glare of the sunlight. He picked up his pace, anxious to draw some distance between himself and the city. Before he'd gone too far, he glanced back over his shoulder for one last look at the dreaded wall, and as he did, a vision flickered across his mind of a decapitated head, the one he'd seen on his first day, caked in blood and covered in flies. Then the face of the stranger disappeared, and instead it was George's head staring blankly out across the land. Daniel blinked and rubbed his eyes, and when he opened them again, the vision was gone. But it had given him a terrible sense of foreboding.

+

The execution site lay beyond the defensive wall, at the foot of a steep hill. The day had grown warm, and the walk was long and arduous. Daniel kept his eyes on the rocky ground as he plodded silently forward amid the sullen crowd, up the steep slope, ever closer to Georges' fate.

By the time he reached the top of the hill, the muscles in his calves had begun to burn, and he'd developed a painful cramp in his side. He stopped for a minute to catch his breath and gaze down at the valley floor below. It was then that he caught his first glimpse of the execution site. Hundreds of people had already begun to gather around it, and still more were flowing in from all directions. Some had climbed into nearby trees in order to get a good view. Several horses and imperial carriages were tethered to a clump of trees along the fringes. The governor was there, standing alone in the shade of a large chestnut tree while all around him dozens of clerks and slaves moved about, setting up chairs, reading over scrolls, tending to the horses…and of course there were soldiers, countless soldiers. But there was only one person on Daniel's mind as his eyes swept over the scene, and with a lurch of his stomach, he soon spotted him being led into the centre of the clearing, half-hidden between two armed guards. The longer that Daniel stood there, gazing down at Georges tiny figure surrounded by an army of red and silver, the more helpless and hopeless he felt. What could he do?

Pasicrates and Deacon Adrian continued to move forward, down the hill, but he remained rooted to his spot, staring down at the scene below, until finally Perpetua appeared and clasped his hand tightly in her own, and when he looked into her sad green eyes he recognized the fear and vulnerability that lay hidden in their depths and knew that she, at least, understood how he felt.

Together they wound their way down the hill, through the crowd, not stopping until at last they found a spot at the front of the throng, less than twenty feet from where George stood, with his head bowed and his eyes closed in silent prayer. He was oblivious to their presence and to all of the hundreds of eyes staring down at him. A few feet behind him, a tall soldier stood waiting. Daniel poured his eyes over him, studying him, taking in every inch, from his shiny helmet to his faded leather shoes, and eventually coming to rest on his sword, the instrument of death. He looked up into the soldiers face. He was curious about this man, the executioner. He wondered how he felt. But there was nothing in the man's face that betrayed any emotion. It was blank. His eyes showed no remorse, no hatred. He was doing his job; that was all.

Daniel closed his eyes. All this time he'd been so certain that he was supposed to do something, that he had a role to play, but what? He rubbed his forehead with the tips of his fingers. *It just doesn't make any sense!* he thought in frustration. *I don't understand! Where's the dragon?*

Suddenly the crowd began to quiet down, and he looked up. The clerks had moved to their seats, and the governor was stepping forward, his long traveling cloak billowing in the wind. He stopped directly beside George and gazed out over the crowd with a look that commanded silence. A gentle breeze rustled in the nearby trees. Someone coughed in the distance. Daniel and Perpetua stood together in the front row, waiting with abated breath. Next to them, Deacon Adrian wrapped his arm comfortingly around Juliana whose hands were clasped tightly in front of her tear-streaked face and whose lips moved in fervent, silent prayer.

"We all know why we're here," bellowed the governor. "This man has been asked repeatedly to make a sacrifice to the gods, and has thus far refused." An angry murmur swept through the audience. George stood calmly next to the governor, with his head held high, his face expressionless. Slowly, the governor began to circle him, his eyes passing over every inch of his tortured body. "You are an enigma, tribune," he said quietly, more to himself than to George, "to have survived —" He stopped abruptly and shook his head, determined to rid his mind, once and for all, of the uneasy thoughts and nagging doubts that had been plaguing him all week. He'd heard the talk in the streets; they were already attributing miracles to the young tribune, calling him a saint. Of course he knew that it was impossible, ridiculous, yet as he gazed into George's face he couldn't help but wonder why someone with so much talent and potential would be willing to throw it all away…and the old doubts began to resurface. He closed his eyes and firmly reminded himself that, despite his own misgivings, the emperor had made his decision. Christianity was forbidden, and the tribune must suffer the consequences. Unless…

He looked hopefully into George's face and cleared his throat. "I have been ordered to carry out your sentence," he said loudly, hoping that the audience could see that he was a fair and reasonable man, "but before I do, I beseech you one last time to reconsider and to make a simple offering."

George shook his head. "I am Christian," he said simply.

"Be sane, man!" begged the governor. "Pay homage to the gods! It is an offence to offend them!"

"I worship the all-powerful and ever-living God," said George. "I have no fear of your gods."

The governor clenched his fists and gritted his teeth in frustration. "Then you shall die!" he threatened.

George narrowed his eyes and, for the first time, looked directly into those of the governor's. "What would you have me do? Quake and bend down and lick the boots of *your* Lord and Master, Gaius Valerius Aurelius Diocletianus?"

"He has the power to snuff out your life," hissed the governor.

George's brown eyes stared piercingly into those of the governor's. "Yes," he said calmly, "so he has, but that doesn't change who I am." Then he turned and looked out over the watchful crowd. "I am Christian," he said loudly, "and I am a soldier. I've spent my entire life fighting for Rome, faithfully serving my emperor," he threw the governor a hard stare, "yet here I am." The governor's eyes shifted uncomfortably to a group of by-standing soldiers as George continued. "In my darkest hour, I kneeled before the Lord, and I asked him, 'Why God? Why?'" The enraptured crowd was now so silent that even those seated halfway up the grassy slopes of the hillside could hear his voice. "And my prayers were answered, and my mission is clear. I am a soldier of Christ now!"

The crowd went wild. "Pray for me, George!" they cried. "Don't kill him, kill me instead!" And as they cheered and wept and prayed for God's mercy, George turned back to the governor. "Do with me what you will," he said quietly.

The governor was speechless. He twisted his hands together and opened his mouth to speak but then closed it and instead spun around and marched over to his seat. Like bees on honey, his well-paid clerks and advisors swarmed around him, speaking in hushed voices.

Next to Daniel, Perpetua fell to her knees and buried her face in her hands, weeping bitterly. At the sound of her wailing, George looked over at them and his expression softened.

"Oh Pet," he whispered, "I'm so sorry…" He wanted to say more, to tell them how much he loved them, and that everything would be all right, but his heart was heavy and his body weak. Unable to bear the sight of their sorrowful faces, he bowed his head, closed his eyes, and prayed that it would soon be over.

Soon the clerks broke away from the governor and shuffled back to their seats. A nervous hush fell over the crowd. Reluctantly, the governor rose to his feet and gave the executioner a nod.

As the executioner moved into place, George turned to the governor. "Before I die, may I have one final prayer?"

"You may," he assented.

Through watery eyes, Daniel watched George kneel and bow his head. *This is it,* he thought miserably, *it's really going to happen.* He closed his eyes and whispered a feverish prayer under his breath and, in so doing, unconsciously reached for his cross, squeezing it in desperation. Suddenly he was seized with an idea. *Of course!* he thought excitedly. *Why didn't I think of it sooner? It's all so clear now! The cross belongs to George! Didn't Grandpa say so? I must give it to him!* And without hesitation, he rushed forward to the place where George knelt. The fact that there were armed guards stationed everywhere no longer mattered, nor that the governor of Bithynia was standing less than twenty feet away, nor even that the cross was most assuredly his only means of returning home, to the place and the people that he loved most in this world. At that moment in time, Daniel was so certain of his purpose that nothing else mattered. It wasn't that he'd forgotten about the importance of the cross in his own life; in fact, as he rushed forward and tore it over his head, he felt a deep sadness sweep over him — for the loss of his mother and father, the loss of his grandma and grandpa, the farm, his comfortable suburbia home — but he was willing to give it all up for George because his need was greater. And in the back of his mind, a small piece of him hoped beyond hope that the cross would rescue George from this place and take him away from here, to a different time and place. That's really what Daniel was hoping for as he ran forward and fell on his knees before George.

The soldier reached out his arm but was called back by a sharp command from the governor. He would allow the boy to come forward with his offering, why not? What harm could there be in it? It was, after all, only a cross.

"What is it, Daniel?" asked George.

"The cross," he said, holding it forward in his outstretched hands, "it's yours, I mean, I want you to have it." George looked from the cross to Daniel's eager face and back again. It was a thing of rare beauty, this cross, not because of the way its smooth surface shone in the sunlight but because of everything it represented and the hope that it conveyed. He reached out and touched it.

"Are you sure?" he asked. Daniel nodded and slung the cross gently over his head. George turned it over in his good hand and read the inscription on the back. "Trust in the Lord and do good," he murmured. "Trust in the Lord...."

"Words to live by," whispered Daniel, remembering his grandfather's wise words.

George smiled into his tear-streaked face. "Remember me, Daniel," he said. "Promise me you'll remember me."

"Of course," choked Daniel, "always..." He stumbled back into the crowd, barely aware of what he was doing, and fell on his knees among strangers.

George looked out over the weeping crowd and smiled bravely. "Take heart," he called, "for this is not the end, but rather the beginning." Then he kissed the cross gently, nodded to the executioner, and bowed his head.

Daniel held his breath as the executioner drew his sword from its sheath and stepped into position. He watched, terrified, as the sword was raised high in the air

and as the sun glittered on the falling blade—and it was
done.
>   But on his breast a bloody cross he bore,
>   The dear remembrance of his dying Lord...*

---

* Catholic Encyclopedia, "St. George", (Edmund Spenser, *The Faerie Queene*) http://www.newadvent.org/cathen/06453a.htm

(XXIV)

"Nooooo!" Daniel covered his eyes with his hands and was engulfed in silence. The only sound was that of his own heart pounding painfully in his chest. Wetness began to seep through the knees of his jeans, but he was oblivious to it. Who knows how long he lay there crying hot tears into the cold, hard earth — seconds…minutes…hours…it could have been an eternity.

"Daniel?! Daniel?!" A familiar voice called out to him through the darkness, pulling him back, and before he knew it, two strong, calloused hands had reached out and lifted him to his feet. And he was looking into his grandfather's worried face.

"Daniel, are you ok?"

"He's dead, Grandpa!" sobbed Daniel. "They killed him! He's dead…"

Grandpa tightened his grip on his grandson's shoulders. "Who's dead?" he asked fearfully.

Daniel took a deep breath and stared into his eyes, willing him to understand. "George," he whispered, "St. George."

His grandfather looked intently into his sorrowful face, as though searching for answers in it. It was then that he spotted the cross dangling from around his neck, and comprehension slowly dawned on him. "Yes," he murmured, drawing Daniel into a comforting embrace. "Yes, he is." They stood like that for several moments, the freezing rain battering down upon them, until finally Grandpa loosened his grip and steered Daniel back down the path, toward the warmth and safety of the farmhouse. Once inside, Daniel allowed himself to be stripped of his wet boots and jacket and plunked into a soft chair in front of the woodstove. He shook his damp hair out of his eyes, threw a blanket around his shoulders, and gazed numbly around the room as his grandfather stoked the fire and quietly prepared two steaming cups of tea. Everything looked the same, yet different.

Eventually, Grandpa sat down in the chair opposite him and handed him his tea. "Well?" he said. "Are you ready to talk about it?"

Daniel nodded. "I was there," he said. "I went back in time. I met George...and..." He was at a loss for words. How could he explain everything that had happened? Who would ever believe him? He squeezed his cross in silence. Finally, his Grandpa spoke.

"Your great-grandfather told me all about St. George. The way that he suffered and died. He was a very brave man. You're lucky to have met him." Daniel nodded and wiped fresh tears from his eyes. After a moment of silence, he spoke again.

"Grandpa," he said, "if you knew the truth about him, why didn't you tell me? Why the story about the dragon? I kept expecting him to save the day by slaying a dragon, but that never happened. Instead it was him that was killed. I don't understand."

"I know it doesn't seem like it," said Grandpa, "but the legend of St. George and the dragon *is* actually true, in a way. It's allegorical."

"Alle...what?" said Daniel.

Grandpa chuckled softly. "An allegory is a story that's meant to be understood symbolically."

"Oh," said Daniel, "so the dragon is really...?"

"The dragon is symbolic of evil, and the princess symbolizes the Church. Emperor Diocletian and Galerius Caesar wanted to wipe out Christianity, but George, along with many other very brave people, stood up to them and won."

"But George never won," argued Daniel. "He died. They killed him."

"Ahhhh, but that's not true," said Grandpa, "not really. In the end George did win. Do you know what happened after he died?" Daniel shook his head. "What you witnessed was the beginning of the Great Persecution," said Grandpa. "It raged for ten long years. It was a dark time for Christians; many men, women, and children suffered for their faith. But finally, in the year 313, it all came to an end when Constantine rose to power and granted Christians the freedom to worship as they please."

"Constantine!?" said Daniel. "I saw him! He came to warn George about the edicts. His father was caesar in the west, wasn't he?"

"Yes, but his father died shortly after the persecutions began, and after his father's death, Constantine fought long and hard to gain the title of emperor. His enemies were many. Diocletian soon retired from political life, but Galerius Caesar wasn't the only one with his sights set on the throne. There were others. Finally, in the year 312 Constantine fought a famous battle on the outskirts of Rome, at the Milvian Bridge, and was declared victorious. It's a fascinating story and has been described as one of the most important events in the history of western civilization.

According to ancient sources, on the day before battle Constantine looked up into the sky and saw a vision of a cross brilliantly imposed over the sun and with it the words, "In this sign you shall conquer." He went to bed that night puzzling over the meaning of his vision and, while he and his troops lay sleeping, had a dream telling him to draw the symbol of the chi-rho on the shields of his men.

In the morning, before going into battle, they did so, and although they were greatly outnumbered, they won. Soon after, Constantine issued an edict ending the persecution against Christians and declaring religious freedom to everyone."

"Just like George wanted," whispered Daniel.

"Yes," said Grandpa, "and Constantine was the first Roman emperor to be baptized. So you see, George did slay the dragon, didn't he." Daniel nodded. "I like to think of the dragon as being symbolic of the evil that we are all faced with, throughout our lives," said Grandpa, "and that like George, if we cling to our faith in God, we too will be able to overcome it."

"I see what you mean now; the story isn't meant to be interpreted literally."

"That's right," said Grandpa. "There are many good books that aren't meant to be interpreted literally." He rose from his chair and drained the rest of his tea. "Are you ok now?" he asked. "You should probably try and get some rest." Daniel nodded but didn't budge. Instead he continued to stare absent-mindedly at the fire in the woodstove. "Is there something else?" asked Grandpa.

Daniel looked up at the sound of his voice. "No, not really," he said. "I was just thinking...what if no one believes me, about George, I mean."

"Just tell the truth," said Grandpa, "that's all that you can do. People will believe what they want to believe. Come on now," he insisted, "sleep will do you good." Daniel rose from his seat and allowed his grandfather to lead him out of the warm kitchen and down the hall toward the foot of the stairs. Before heading in the direction of his own bedroom, Grandpa gave him one last look and shook his head, grinning. "Boy, your grandmother's going to have a heart attack when she sees your hair," he said.

Daniel smiled. "Yeah. Just wait 'til mom sees me."

He swung open the door to his bedroom and peered into the darkness. His first thought was that he wished he had a lamp to see by, but then he remembered what year it was. Blindly, he ran his hand along the smooth wall in search of the switch hoping that the power had been restored, and a second later, with an easy flick, the room was flooded in light. He squinted into the brightness and gazed around himself, surprised to find everything just as he'd left it. There wasn't even any dust. With a slight pang, he noticed the book that he'd been reading, still lying open on the bed. He remembered how anxious he'd been to try and figure out how George had died. Well, he knew now.

Before climbing into bed, he kneeled on the hard floor, bowed his head and prayed—for St. George, Bishop

Anthimus*, St. Perpetua**, and the countless others who suffered and died for their faith.

---

* Bishop Anthimus took refuge in a nearby village and wrote encouraging letters to the Christians of Nicomedia. When the emperor's soldiers found him, he invited them in, fed them a meal and talked with them awhile before allowing them to lead him to his martyrdom.
** St. Perpetua was martyred in 203 A.D. at the age of twenty-two. Her orphaned child was left in the care of her grieving, pagan father.

APRIL 23, 303 A.D.

Under the cover of darkness, a tall, slim man with long dark hair and a grey streaked beard silently approached the arched gate to the city of Nicomedia. Not far away, a fire burned, and three armed soldiers sat warming themselves by it. Although he worked silently, he had no real fear of them, not because he was bold but because he knew each of them by name, had shared a special meal with them and had called them brother. They knew that he was there. Still, he needed to work quickly because there were many other enemies lurking about. He was glad to find the ladder leaning in the proper spot. Deftly, he climbed up and cut loose the bloody, decapitated head. When he reached the ground again, he wrapped it carefully in a blanket and hurried off into the darkness where others were anxiously waiting for him.

"Have you got it?" whispered a man with unruly black hair.

"Yes," he replied, glancing nervously over his shoulder to be sure that he wasn't followed.

Before mounting his horse, he checked over his things to make sure that nothing had been forgotten. "The cross?" he whispered hoarsely to his dark haired companion. "Have you got it?" The man nodded and handed him a satchel containing a small silver cross and chain, which he tucked safely next to his heart. Then he climbed up onto his horse and shook the dust from his feet.

The small group of men journeyed all night long and, by sunrise, made it to the coast where a ship was waiting. Once there, the servant parted from his brothers. He would make the long journey to Lydda, Palestine alone and there grant the last dying wish of his master...his friend...his brother. He would lay him to rest in the proper Christian way, in the land of his ancestors.

A PARTIAL BIBLIOGRAPHY

E.W. Brooks, *Acts of St. George*
J.G.Davies, *Daily Life in the Early Church*
Eusebius, *The Church History*
Eusebius, *The Martyrs in Palestine*
Edward Gibbon, *The Decline and Fall of the Roman Empire*
Lactantius, *Of the Manner in which the Persecutors Died*
Arthur James Mason, *The Persecution of Diocletian*
Edmund Spencer, *The Faerie Queene*
www.earlychristianwritings.com, *The Didache*
The Teaching Company, Professor Bart D. Ehrman, *From Jesus to Constantine: A History of Early Christianity*
The Teaching Company, Professor Garrett G. Fagan, *Emperors of Rome*
The Teaching Company, Professor Kenneth W. Harl, *The Fall of the Pagans and the Origins of Medieval Christianity*